CRUSADER'S
QUEST

BOOKS BY JAKE TYSON

JAKE TYSON

THE VINDICATORS PREQUEL

CRUSADER'S
QUEST

AMBASSADOR INTERNATIONAL
GREENVILLE, SOUTH CAROLINA & BELFAST, NORTHERN IRELAND

www.ambassador-international.com

Crusader's Quest

Paperback ISBN: 978-1-64960-435-4
eISBN: 978-1-64960-483-5
Library of Congress Control Number: 2024933859

Cover design by Hannah Linder Designs
Interior Typesetting by Dentelle Design
Edited by Allison Wells

AMBASSADOR INTERNATIONAL
Emerald House
411 University Ridge, Suite B14
Greenville, SC 29601
United States
www.ambassador-international.com

AMBASSADOR BOOKS
The Mount
2 Woodstock Link
Belfast, BT6 8DD
Northern Ireland, United Kingdom
www.ambassadormedia.co.uk

The colophon is a trademark of Ambassador, a Christian publishing company.

NINE MONTHS BEFORE
VIGILANTE'S LIGHT . . .

CHAPTER 1

Rain pattered against the grocery store window, beading into droplets that trickled gently down to the metal sill below. It was a gentle rain, nothing more than a refreshing shower. No peals of thunder warned of an oncoming storm, no frantic pedestrians hurrying to find shelter before the worst of the downpour began.

That was, in part, because precious few pedestrians loitered on the streets of the Brooks once the sun went down behind the distant hills, anyway. Once, the Brooks had been a peaceful, pleasant place to live. Sojourn City had been built that way, a social experiment of sorts to see if the intermingling of rich and poor could create a harmonious living environment.

But inevitably, greed and pride got in the way. The rich drifted further and further toward the shores of Lake Superior. Many of them retreated entirely to the Platform, a manmade island that was connected to Sojourn City by a bridge which could retract as some idealistic fool's plan to cast off the wealthy should they become a problem. The Platform had been built to protect the lower classes from the machinations of the wealthy, but it had instead become a luxurious retreat for the one percent.

When the one-percenters saw the rising crime rates that inevitably followed their departure, they feared the criminal elements in the Brooks would spread to Sojourn City's wealthier neighborhoods. Many of them started paying off the police; and the majority of officers drifted closer to the shore, leaving the Brooks all but abandoned. Only the brave men and women of the twelfth precinct remained.

So, the Brooks festered. Criminals ruled the night. No one would go out if they knew what was good for them.

Wyatt Jonson was not afraid. He had a family that needed caring. Joanna had sent him out for a few groceries after he got home from work, and he was determined to get everything that his wife and children needed. There was no point in living life in fear. Anyone who let terror control them was living no life at all, in Wyatt's opinion.

He did not like the condition of the Brooks—sex traffickers, drug dealers, gangs aplenty—but he would endure. He had to. He and his family were on hard times. Wyatt's job as a factory worker did not pay nearly enough money for him to move them out of the Brooks, let alone out of Sojourn City. So, for the foreseeable future, they would remain where they were, in a slum of plummeting property values and greedy landlords. Wyatt was not scared for himself. He was a big man, muscular and intimidating. He could take care of himself.

Despite his determination not to fear, though, he did worry for his children. Carter was almost seventeen, and it would be easy for him to fall prey to the temptations of joining a gang. The Red Dogs and the Tyrants tried to snatch up every teenage boy that hit the streets. The thought of Carter becoming a gangster—or even being mistaken for one by an overzealous police officer—was terrifying. Ellis and Rhonda were even younger, and Wyatt had recurring nightmares of them walking home from school and being caught in the crossfire of a gang shootout. But they could not escape the Brooks. It was their home, and for the time being, their prison.

Wyatt scooped up the last of the items on Joanna's list into his shopping basket and weaved through the aisles toward the cash register. The sooner he got home to his family and locked the doors behind him, the better.

The cashier was a timid-looking man with a slender frame and uncombed brown hair. Bags hung under his bloodshot eyes. Wyatt tried not to be judgmental—he knew what it was like to be on the receiving end of such judgment—but between the bloodshot eyes and the trembling hands, he suspected the man before him was in withdrawal from some illicit substance.

Wyatt smiled at the man. "Good evening."

Sometimes, someone withdrawing from drugs just needed to see a friendly face. Wyatt hoped the man was withdrawing because he was trying to shake his habit and not because he couldn't afford another fix. Either way, he needed to know that someone out there cared about him as a person.

"H-hi." The man's eyes widened slightly, and he started taking items from Wyatt's basket to scan them. "Find everything okay?"

Wyatt caught a glimpse of his own reflection in the convex mirror above the register, and he understood why the cashier had looked frightened. Wyatt's muscular frame, combined with his neatly trimmed goatee and close-cropped hair, gave him an intimidating air. Besides that, his years in the army made him carry himself like a soldier. Wyatt looked like a force to be reckoned with, even wearing a white jersey and a navy blue hoodie. He supposed the cashier had been sizing up Wyatt just as Wyatt had sized him up.

"Sure did." Wyatt made an effort to keep his voice light. The last thing he wanted was to spook the man. "Good thing, too. Gotta keep the missus happy, right? On a rainy night like this, I don't want to be sleeping on the porch."

The cashier forced a chuckle. "Definitely not."

Despite the insincerity of his laugh, the cashier's tense shoulders slackened. He stopped rushing and scanned the items more deliberately. Apparently, he had decided that Wyatt wasn't a threat. *Mission accomplished.* Wyatt reached into the pocket of his jeans and scooped out his wallet. By the time his last item was scanned in, he owed just over twenty dollars. He cringed at the amount but handed the cashier two tens and a handful of quarters.

"Steep," he said.

The cashier nodded. "Y-you know how it is. Times are tough for everyone."

"No doubt about that."

Wyatt deposited the handful of pennies he got in change into the small tray next to the register. The next customer might need them more than he did. Wyatt took the bagged groceries from the cashier, wished him a good night, and headed out into the rain. He pulled his hood up before stepping out onto the sidewalk. It was a short walk back to his car, but he would rather keep as dry as possible.

Thud. Thud.

Wyatt recognized the dull striking sound of knuckles against flesh and bone all too well. His stomach sank. Someone was getting a beatdown.

A scream echoed from the alley to Wyatt's left. He froze. His car was just ahead on the other side of the street. He could cross over, get in, ignore the cry. *Keep your head down.* It was none of his business.

Crack.

"Help me!"

Wyatt sighed. He was a soldier. He had never been very good at keeping his head down. He set his bag of groceries down as close to the building as he could. Maybe the slight overhang would keep them from getting drenched, at least. Then, zipping up his hoodie, he stepped into the alley.

CHAPTER 2

There were two men in the alley. One was sitting in a puddle with his back against the brick wall, his arm raised to shield his face. Blood and rainwater ran down his cheek from his temple. The other man stood over him, brandishing a length of pipe and shouting at his victim to shut up. The assailant wore a red bomber jacket. In this neighborhood, a red jacket was almost always a sign that the wearer belonged to the Red Dogs gang. If he was a Red Dog, he probably had friends nearby.

It didn't matter. An innocent man was being hurt, and Wyatt was the only one around to stop it. As the thug raised the pipe for another blow, Wyatt clenched his fists, popped his knuckles, and strode into the alley. He made his frame as big as he could, squaring his shoulders and spreading his feet.

"Hey!"

The thug stopped at the shout and turned. For a second, his eyes were wide—no doubt, he had expected that a police officer would be the only person brave enough to intervene. When he saw that he was wrong, his eyes narrowed again, and he patted the pipe against his empty palm.

"Get out of here." The thug stepped forward. "This ain't none of your business."

Wyatt licked his lips. "Leave the man alone."

He hoped the darkness of the alley and the depth of his hood were enough to hide his face from the thug. The last thing he needed was to be identified as an enemy of the Red Dogs. Still, he could not leave the other man to be robbed or die. It was a stupid move, and Joanna would never let him hear the end of it if she found out; but someone had to do something. Wyatt had the training to be the one.

"I said step off, big man." The thug was only three steps away. "You're lucky I'm in a forgiving mood. Leave, and I'll forget you went temporarily insane."

"Can't do that."

The victim saw his chance. With the Red Dog distracted, the bleeding man leaped from the ground and sprinted the other way, his shoes splashing in rain puddles all the way down the alley. The Red Dog turned, watched his target flee, and swore under his breath. When he turned back to Wyatt, there was a new fire in his eyes.

"You just cost me tomorrow's lunch money. Guess I'll have to take it from you, instead."

The Red Dog swung. Wyatt stepped back, leaning his head away so the pipe missed his skull. He lurched in before the Red Dog completed his swing. Pinning the thug's arm against his body, Wyatt swung a right cross, cracking his fist against the Red Dog's jaw. The thug reeled, spat on the rough pavement, and shook his head.

"I was just gonna rob you. Now, it looks like I have to kill you."

Wyatt extended a hand and waved his fingers toward himself.

With a guttural roar, the thug charged. Wyatt dodged his first swing and took the second to his bicep. Pain exploded up and down his arm. The thug followed up with a punch that struck Wyatt's chin, clacking his teeth together and swelling his lip. Panic frazzled

Wyatt's brain as he took two long step backs, seeking distance from his opponent.

Don't fear. Act. He clenched his fists. *Make* him *scared.*

As the thug launched his next attack, Wyatt did not defend. He ducked under the blow and charged in, wrapping his arms around the Red Dog's waist and taking him to the ground. Wyatt buried his head in the Red Dog's chest to protect his face. He rained down wild blows on the thug, even as he received a few across the back of his head and shoulders. The pipe clattered to the ground somewhere. Wyatt struck twice more, then pulled back and kicked the pipe out of the thug's reach. Wheezing, the gang member hauled himself to his feet and raised his fists.

Wyatt blocked the next punch. And the next. He boxed his opponent's ears, roundhouse kicked him back into the wall, and drove his elbow into the man's chin. The Red Dog spit a tooth and a stream of blood. Wyatt's fingers trembled, but he forced them still. He had to remain focused until he knew the fight was over.

"You think . . . you've accomplished something?" The Red Dog sneered. "Beating up one Red Dog won't stop us from controlling the Brooks."

"Maybe. But I saved one man."

"That'll never . . . be enough . . . "

Wyatt shrugged. As far as he could tell, the thug was done fighting. Wyatt took a step back toward the entrance of the alley. He backed up until he was five paces distant from the thug before he turned on his heel. He hoped no one had taken his groceries in the time he had spent fighting.

Something grabbed him from behind and tugged him back. Wyatt's hood came free. He spun and punched. The thug's nose crumpled beneath Wyatt's knuckles. The Red Dog howled and wiped tears from his eyes, but he glared spitefully back at Wyatt.

"I've seen your face now." The thug swallowed. "We know who to look for."

A cold, unfamiliar knife buried itself in Wyatt's soul. If the Red Dog went back to his gang and told them what had happened, Wyatt would land at the top of their target list. He was not safe; and worse, neither was his family. Carter, Ellis, Rhonda—his kids were in danger. So was Joanna.

Wyatt surged forward and kicked the Red Dog in the gut. The man doubled over; and Wyatt grabbed him, spun him around, and locked him in a chokehold. The fear in Wyatt's heart burrowed further. It was not fear for his family now because he would do whatever it took to make sure they were safe. It was fear of what he was about to do.

"You're right," Wyatt said. "And because of that . . . I'm sorry . . . I can't let you tell anyone. Ever."

"Hey . . . " the thug gasped. "Don't . . . "

Wyatt adjusted his grip, just like he had learned in the army. It would be quick—not easy, certainly, but he had the muscle, the leverage, the training. He knew what to do. It was the only choice he had. He wondered if he would ever forgive himself.

In one fluid motion, he snapped the Red Dog's neck.

"I'm so sorry." Tears streamed down his cheeks as Wyatt let the man's body fall to the rain-drenched alley floor. "But no one will ever touch my family."

CHAPTER 3

He was grateful that the kids were all in bed when he got home. If they had seen him in his present condition . . . Wyatt shuddered. His children had never looked at him with fear in their eyes, and he was determined that they would not start now. He was their father, their protector, their friend. He would never give them cause to be scared of him.

Joanna, on the other hand, was terrified.

After setting the groceries down on the kitchen table, Wyatt had hurried to the bathroom. Joanna had seen him from the living room and rushed after. She gasped when she saw the blood and bruises but managed to keep quiet so she wouldn't wake the kids. Now, they stood together in the bathroom as Wyatt scrubbed blood from his knuckles.

"It was all a big mistake." Wyatt rinsed his mouth, letting blood flow down into the basin. "I saw a man in trouble . . . being mugged in an alley. I couldn't just let it happen. No one else was around. It had to be me. It was dark, and I had my hood up. I thought . . . I thought I could help."

Joanna's lips curved upward in a sad smile. "That's my husband. Always the hero."

"Hero." Wyatt scoffed. "Hardly. While I was fighting the thug, he pulled my hood off. He saw my face and threatened . . ." A lump rose in his throat. He choked back a sob. "If he told his friends who I was, they would've found us. They would've hurt you or the kids. I couldn't let that happen. I didn't want to do it. After I came home from overseas, I thought I'd never have to . . . I thought those days were over. But the thought of the Red Dogs coming after us was too much. I . . . " Tears streamed down Wyatt's face. "I killed him."

She was quiet after that. Wyatt focused on cleaning himself because he couldn't bear to look at her. What if she wore an expression of disgust? What if she didn't recognize the man she had married? He had killed many people in war, some that he was ashamed of; but killing a man in an alley was something else entirely. This was home. He was supposed to be safe here.

Joanna's hand rested on his shoulder. "You did what you thought was right at that moment."

"He's dead. Dead, Jo. How could I do that?"

"You were protecting the ones you loved." Her grip tightened. "It was a horrible thing, but it sounds like he left you no choice. You were trying to do a good thing, and it went south. What matters is you're okay. You're here. The Red Dogs will never know it was you."

That much was true, thankfully. And even though that Red Dog was dead, his victim had escaped. He had received a blow to the head; but otherwise, he was no worse for wear. Wyatt had to admit, if not for killing the man, it would have felt good. He had saved someone. If only he could have done it without killing.

"I know you're right, Jo. It's just . . . it's going to take some time to process."

She took his hands, pulled him around to face her, and brought his clasped hands up to rest beneath her chin. There was no fear in her eyes. No revulsion. Relief swept through Wyatt, but it was still mitigated by his own guilt and self-disgust. Her view of him had not changed, but his view of himself . . .

"Maybe it's time you talk to that pastor," she said.

Wyatt's jaw tightened. He had been a churchgoer once, but that had been long ago. In recent months, two new churches had opened in the Brooks, both offshoots of Refuge Church over in Lakeside. The pastor of the nearer campus, a red-haired man named Jeff, had invited Wyatt and Joanna to their services. Wyatt had been hesitant to go, but Joanna was right. There was no one better to discuss guilt than a man of God.

"I will." Wyatt finished washing his hands and then dried them on a towel. "First thing tomorrow, I'll go down to the church and talk with him."

"Good. Now, no more of this tonight. You need your rest. Let's go to bed."

Wyatt pulled his wife into a hug. "Thank you. I . . . I was afraid you'd never look at me the same once you knew. I'm not a murderer, Jo. I didn't want to be. I swear, I'll never take another life if I can help it."

"I know, baby. I know. But you don't have to stop helping people. Please, never do that. Because then, you wouldn't be the man I fell in love with."

Wyatt tightened his grip around her and cried into her shoulder.

* * *

With the sunlight came some relief. An immense weight of guilt remained, like an industrial refrigerator resting on his chest, but the night was over. He had taken a life, something he would have to carry forever, but he had killed before. It was in the past. All he could do was move forward and do his best to atone for it.

At least, Joanna had given him a way to unburden himself. Confessing to her had already alleviated some of his guilt, and he hoped that talking with that pastor would be a greater help. In his childhood, Wyatt had gone to church with his grandmother every Sunday. He was no stranger to religion or faith. He had grown distant from God and the church, though, since his tenure in the army. Going back felt almost like admitting defeat. He would have to confess that he had not felt church was important enough. That would be embarrassing enough, but then to tell the pastor that he had killed a man . . .

Wyatt swallowed. He had no other choice. If he kept this guilt bottled up, it would eat him alive from the inside out.

He dressed in his work coveralls and groomed his goatee. Joanna was down the hall making breakfast for him and the kids. The school bus would arrive soon, taking them off to another day where Wyatt could only hope the greatest dangers they faced were intimidating tests and mouthy bullies. In the Brooks, coming away from school with encounters like that was more blessing than burden.

Wyatt snapped the last buttons on his coveralls together and stepped out of the bathroom. Footsteps clomped on the stairs; and Ellis and Rhonda darted for the kitchen, sparing their dad a wave and a "Hi!" as they passed. Wyatt cracked a smile, perhaps for the first time since the previous night's incident, and crossed his arms to lean against the kitchen door jamb. Behind him, more feet tapped on the stairway, these slower and more precise than the frantic sprinting of the younger two Jonson children.

Carter sidled up to his father. He was already nearly as tall as Wyatt and not done growing yet. He had broad shoulders that almost matched his father's and an impressive muscle tone for a kid his age.

Carter was on the school wrestling team, just as Wyatt had been in his high school years. Now that his tall, lanky frame was filling out, Carter was becoming devastatingly handsome. Something that, once again, Wyatt would have liked to take credit for, he thought with a wry smile.

"Hey, Dad." Carter frowned, an expression all too common for him recently. "I thought I heard crying last night." He paused as his gaze took in Wyatt's injuries. "What happened?"

"Don't worry, son." He cleared his throat. It wasn't unusual for Wyatt to come home with a bruise or two after a strenuous day at work. He hoped he could play off his injuries as the result of a particularly grueling shift. "Got into a bit of an accident at work last night, but I'm fine. So is your mom."

"Is everyone else?"

Sharp as a whip, this kid. Carter was fiercely protective, not just of his younger siblings but also of his parents. Part of the reason Wyatt did not worry more about his children was because he was confident that Carter would do everything in his might to protect the younger two from all kinds of danger. But Carter was also impulsive, brash. Of the three, Wyatt worried most about him, even though he was the strongest. Wyatt feared that one day, he might get himself into a situation he could not punch his way out of.

"We're all okay." Wyatt clapped his hand down on Carter's shoulder and squeezed. "The world just gets heavy sometimes, that's all. Crying can be a good outlet to shed some of that weight. Don't worry. There's nothing going on in any of your lives that your mother and I can't handle together."

Carter finally cracked a smile. "Okay. Love you, Dad."

"Love you, too, son."

As Carter stepped into the kitchen to grab his breakfast, Wyatt pressed his lips into a thin line. He hoped he had not just lied to his son. The death of that Red Dog was much bigger than Wyatt felt able to handle alone. Joanna could help him shoulder it; but sooner or later, the truth had to come out. All Wyatt could pray was that when it did, it did not come out to the Red Dogs or the cops.

Wyatt would do what he could to atone for his crimes, but he could not leave his family to go to prison—and he certainly could not face the wrath of the gangs.

CHAPTER 4

It felt wrong to go into a church wearing grime-smeared coveralls, even if it was on a Tuesday and not during service hours. Wyatt brought a change of clothes with him to the factory and changed into a pair of blue jeans and a black, button-down, short-sleeved shirt on his lunch break. The church was only a few miles from the factory; so with any luck, Wyatt could make it there to talk to the pastor and back before his lunch break was over.

Although he was not hungry, he knew he needed to keep full so he would have the energy to continue working the rest of the day. On his drive to the church, he used one hand to unwrap the tuna sandwich Joanna had packed for him. He ate it without really tasting, just chewing and swallowing on autopilot. There were times when Wyatt enjoyed his meals with singular satisfaction. But the burden he carried made any kind of enjoyment seem distant and unreachable.

He finished off the sandwich and ate most of an apple by the time he pulled into the church parking lot. He took the water bottle from his lunch sack and brought it with him. As he mounted the steps leading up to the church's front doors, his legs weighed him down like lead pillars. *I can't do this.* There was always the chance that the pastor would feel obligated to turn Wyatt over to the police. Something urged him on, though. He had to unburden himself.

He pushed through the church's double doors and stepped through the foyer. The sanctuary was lined with light wood benches on either side, leaving the single aisle down the middle leading up to the altar. Wyatt drummed his fingers against his legs. The doors were unlocked, so someone must have been at the church; but he did not know where to look.

Instead of roaming aimlessly, Wyatt stepped into the sanctuary and looked up at the cross mounted on the wall above the stage. Something about the imagery of the cross had always resonated with Wyatt. A device intended for torture and execution, it had instead come to resemble the ultimate hope. How did one redeem that kind of image? *Maybe the same way one redeems the kind of evil I've committed.*

Wyatt took a seat on the rearmost bench on the left side of the sanctuary. He folded his hands, rested them on the back of the bench in front of him, and looked up at the cross.

"What I did was wrong," he said softly. "I know that. But I was trying to protect an innocent man."

He did not know if he was trying to convince God or himself. His intentions had been genuine, and he had not gone in prepared to kill. He had only done so because the Red Dog had seen his face, and that threatened his family. Surely, God understood that Wyatt would never have callously murdered the man needlessly.

"The people in this neighborhood need a protector." Wyatt's voice was barely a whisper. "I-I don't know if that's me; but for that one man, it was. I did what I had to so he could live on. And who am I if not my family's protector? If the Red Dogs had come after them, they all could've died. I never meant to . . . to . . . "

"To what?"

Wyatt jumped at the voice and glanced over his shoulder. The man behind him wore a pair of khakis and a green plaid shirt. He had thinning red hair and a kind face with piercing blue eyes. He was the pastor who had invited Wyatt to attend the church.

Wyatt rose from the bench and fiddled with his hands for a moment before finally extending his right for a handshake. Jeff gripped Wyatt's hand and shook it with a smile. Wyatt lowered his head and studied the tops of Jeff's brown shoes.

"Pastor Jeff." Wyatt cleared his throat. "I'm not sure if you remember me. I'm Wyatt Jonson. You invited my family and me to visit your church."

The pastor nodded. "I do remember. It's good to see you, Wyatt, though I don't get many first-time visitors on Tuesdays. Would you like to be left alone? I know a time of prayer and conversation with God can be a very private thing. If you'd like me to return later or just leave you altogether . . . "

"No." Wyatt gestured to the bench. "I came here to talk to you, actually. Do you have a few minutes?"

"Of course."

Wyatt scooted further down the bench, so Jeff could sit. He was not used to being nervous about any kind of conversation. Wyatt was as straightforward and uncomplicated as they came. He said what he meant and looked whoever he was talking to in the eye when he said it. But at that moment, he found it hard to meet Jeff's gaze.

"I-I have to confess something," he said.

"Well, I'm not a priest, Wyatt. I'm not exactly authorized to take confessions." Jeff smiled as he said it, though, and he put a gentle hand on Wyatt's shoulder. "Anything you need to confess, you can tell straight to God. But I do understand that sometimes telling another person helps ease the conscience."

Wyatt interlaced his fingers and squeezed them until his knuckles whitened. Telling the pastor was risky. There was every chance that Jeff would feel obligated to turn Wyatt over to the police. Yet wasn't confession the reason Wyatt had come to the church? Could he trust that the pastor would keep his deeds in confidence? Perhaps it was a risk he would have to take because the words seemed ready to tumble out of his mouth unbidden.

"I was at the store picking up a few things my wife needed . . . "

He walked through the events of the previous night, explaining how he had seen the man in need and had only wanted to help. He emphasized that his intention had been to leave the thug in the alley once the victim escaped, but the thug had pressed the fight and pulled Wyatt's hood free.

"As soon as he saw my face, I—" Wyatt's voice hitched. He swallowed. "If he had gone back to his gang and told them who I was, my family . . . I couldn't put them in danger. I didn't even really think. I just acted, like I was trained to do in the army. Any life-threatening presence gets put down. So, I did." Tears welled in Wyatt's eyes anew. "I killed him. Broke his neck, right there in the alley, and left his body behind."

Jeff's mouth had drawn into a line, and his brow lowered as Wyatt spoke; but he never looked scared. Wyatt appreciated that. The pastor inhaled deeply through his nose, laced his hands together in his lap, and faced forward. Wyatt hung his head, waiting for the judgment he was sure was coming.

"I know murder is condemned in the Bible," Wyatt said. "I certainly know it's against the law. I won't try to justify it or make excuses. What I did . . . "

"What you did was murder, Wyatt. You're right." Jeff looked over at him. "But I can't say I don't understand your reasoning. The Brooks is a dangerous place to live, and you have children to care for. I myself don't live in the Brooks, even though I pastor here; and my children are grown. Were I in your situation, I probably would have done exactly the same thing."

Wyatt's eyes went wide. He recoiled from the other man, sliding away a few inches in the seat. "But . . . but you're a pastor."

"I'm also a father—and a human being, complete with flaws and fears. Yes, you killed a man, Wyatt, and I wouldn't exactly say it was self-defense, but it . . . well, it was in defense of your family. And the truth is, I heard some of what you were saying before I walked in, and you are right. The Brooks needs a protector. The police are doing their best, but they're undermanned. Their funding is going to the precincts near the Platform, and some of them are corrupt. It's an impossible job."

Pastor Jeff leaned back, resting one of his arms on the back of their bench. "What you did to protect that man was admirable, even if the outcome wasn't desirable. If you confess what you did to God, make it right with Him, who am I to hold you in contempt?"

"Do you think God can forgive me?"

"He forgave the very ones who killed His Son." Jeff shrugged. "I don't see why He can't forgive you, too. All you have to do is ask."

Wyatt looked back at the cross. *He forgave the very ones who killed His Son.* That was more forgiveness than Wyatt would've found in himself. His throat bobbed. Finally, he closed his eyes.

"God, I . . . I'm sorry. You and I—we've been distant for a while now. I've gone my own way, and look where that's led. I'm sorry. Please, if You can forgive me—not just for killing that man but for everything I've done wrong in my whole rough life—I'll try to do better. I'll live the way I know You want me to. But I can't do it without You. I need You here in my life to save me from myself, to change me into a better person, to forgive me. Please, God. Amen."

Jeff reached over and took Wyatt's shoulder again. "I'm very proud of you, Wyatt. That was a brave step. I'm here anytime you need to talk, and we would love for your family to visit on a Sunday."

"We will." Wyatt paused, studied the floor, and then looked back up at Jeff. Next came the moment of truth. His pulse pounded in his throat, and his breaths came short and shallow. "Will you tell the police what I did?"

The pastor took a slow, deep breath. "Some mysteries are better left unsolved. I think this gangster's death might be one of them."

"Thank you."

"You're welcome. Now . . . " Jeff narrowed his eyes. "I really think you and I should talk more about this protector idea."

Wyatt leaned back and raised an eyebrow. "What do you mean?"

"Well, like I said, I think your intentions were good in trying to protect that man. And you yourself said the Brooks needs a protector. You want your kids to grow up in a place where you don't have to fear for their safety, don't you?"

"I-I do, but are you suggesting . . . ?"

"I'm not suggesting anything. I am commenting on the fact that as far as I can tell, the only mistake you made in helping that man was not concealing your identity better. If you had done that, you never would've had to kill the gang member."

"I . . . I guess that's true."

"Just think about it." Jeff rose and started for the door to the foyer. "In times like this, the people need hope. What better hope than someone who protects them in the dead of night? Someone like that could be more than just a hoodlum trading punches in an alley. They could be a symbol."

Wyatt sat back on the bench as Jeff left him alone. His eyes traveled back up to the cross on the front wall. *A symbol.* Maybe Jeff had a point.

CHAPTER 5

The next few days passed in tense anticipation. The burden of guilt on Wyatt's soul had lifted in a tremendous way; and though he still felt the occasional pang of regret, he had learned to accept what he had done and forgive himself. Still, he lived in fear of a knock on the door from police officers with a warrant for his arrest.

By passing the alley on the way home from the church, Wyatt had been able to eavesdrop on the police officers on the scene. A detective named Simon Walters had been assigned to the case. Wyatt hoped that the rain had washed away any traces of his DNA or fingerprints on the Red Dog's body. Since then, he had avoided traveling that street for any reason.

He kept his head down as the days drew on, waiting for word on the results of the investigation. The kids did not know what was going on, but Carter noticed better than the other two that Wyatt was not quite himself. Wyatt reminded his eldest son again and again that he did not have to worry about protecting his parents. Wyatt and Joanna could handle what was going on, and everything was all right.

But as Wyatt watched the news each night, he realized that his words to Carter were a lie. Everything was not all right. The Brooks was getting worse. A shootout between the Red Dogs and the Tyrants caught a retirement home in the crossfire. Cocaine and meth sales were at an all-time high. The one bright side, though it could hardly be called that, was that the Red Dog Wyatt had murdered became one casualty among many. The singular murder investigation became far less important.

The gangs were extorting protection money from every local business struggling to get by. Wyatt had even heard of a few churches being hit. *Maybe that's why Jeff pushed the protector thing so hard.* If Jeff's parishioners were threatened, of course the pastor wanted something to be done. So far, neither Refuge Church had been a target, but Wyatt suspected it was only a matter of time. Every day as Wyatt went to work, it seemed the people on the sidewalks kept their heads hung a little lower.

Joanna was excited that Wyatt was recommitted to God and wanted to start going to church. They planned to go together the following Sunday. Wyatt was open with her and the kids about that decision, but he kept his conversation with Pastor Jeff regarding a protector quiet. He had not decided what to do about that particular issue yet, and he did not want to worry his family for no reason. If the time came when he did decide to follow Jeff's indirect suggestion, he would tell them.

There was no denying that the people around him needed hope. They needed a symbol. Wyatt was not sure he was the one to become that symbol. But if no one else would do it, then he would fill the gap.

On Saturday, he went to Pop's Gym. The gym was a training location for boxers, and it had been a mainstay in the Brooks almost since Sojourn City's founding. If Wyatt was going to become the symbol Jeff had talked about, he needed to polish his skills. His army training was good, but he had been out of the service for many years. He was rusty.

He was going to change that.

Wyatt found a punching bag in the corner, shrugged out of his overshirt, and squared off with the bag. Training with an actual opponent would be more ideal than an inanimate target, but the bag was a decent start. Wyatt could regain his muscle memory, start honing his accuracy, and try to find an opponent to spar with once he was back in a groove.

As he pounded away at the bag, he fell into a rhythm, dodging and weaving in time with an imaginary foe. He pictured all the injustice and heartbreak in the Brooks and made it his enemy, punching relentlessly as though his fists could cure everything wrong with the city he loved. Time stretched until it was meaningless and all that remained was Wyatt, his fists, and the bag.

He punched until his knuckles were sore; until his arms, neck, and forehead beaded with sweat; and until his tank top was drenched with it. Finally, he relaxed. He lowered his guard and unraveled the protective binding around his hands.

"Excuse me." The voice was a rich baritone, only slightly higher in pitch than Wyatt's own deep rumble. "You're Carter Jonson's dad, right?"

Wyatt turned. The man behind him wore a gray tank top and loose black shorts. His skin was dark brown like Wyatt's, and his head was bald. Almost every inch of exposed skin bore a tattoo—a battle ax on his right wrist, barbed wire and a skull on his right bicep and shoulder, a heart with a sword through it just below his collarbone, a band of flame around his left bicep, and a cross on his right shoulder. A scar marred his left cheek just under his eye, and another crossed his scalp on the left side of his head.

The man looked dangerous, powerful. Wyatt instantly recognized a fellow soldier, a man who carried himself with discipline and structure.

But the tattoos, the scars . . . this was a man more dangerous than any soldier Wyatt knew. Still, despite all that, there was a friendly glint in his eyes.

"You know Carter?" Wyatt asked.

The man nodded. "I've met him a couple times in passing. Seen him wrestle, too. I volunteer at his high school, running an after-school program for at-risk youth. The drug epidemic in this city is going to target our young, so I try to cut it off before it gets to them."

"That's a noble goal." Wyatt extended his hand. "Wyatt Jonson."

The man's handshake was firm, vicelike. "Silas Rockwell. I noticed you were going at that bag pretty hard. If you need to hit something that'll fight back, I'm available."

"Thanks. I might just take you up on that." Wyatt gestured to a nearby bench, and he and Silas sat. "Were you a soldier, Silas?"

"Sure was. Just ended my last tour a couple years ago. I'm from Chicago originally, but I moved my family here to Sojourn to find a safer home. Now we're here and . . . "

"And the Brooks probably makes Chicago look like paradise." Wyatt clenched his jaw. "I'm sorry for that. Wouldn't blame you if you took your family and hopped on the next bus out of here."

Silas chuckled. "Don't think I haven't considered it. But . . . I've realized there will be danger anywhere. We can keep running, or we can do something about it and make our home into a place we want our kids to live in."

"Amen to that. How many do you have?"

"Two. Both under the age of three." Silas grinned wryly. "It's a full-time job, keeping up with them."

"I remember those days well. Treasure them while you can."

"I will. Let me see your phone, and I'll put in my number. I figure you're probably done for the day; but if you want to set up a time to meet back here and go a few rounds in the ring, I'm game."

Wyatt handed over his phone. When they had exchanged numbers, Silas stood and shook Wyatt's hand again.

"Good to meet you, Wyatt."

"You, too, Silas."

As the other man walked away, Wyatt gathered his belongings. Silas' words echoed in his head. *We can keep running, or we can do something about it.* They mirrored Wyatt's own thoughts, not to mention Jeff's words at the church. More and more, signs were appearing that Wyatt could not ignore. He had ignored the problem long enough. It was time to do something.

CHAPTER 6

Like many other children, Wyatt had enjoyed reading comic books when he was a boy. Growing up in the eighties, he had his pick of the lot when it came to superheroes. He had even been fortunate enough to see heroes that looked like him—among them men like Black Lightning and John Stewart, the Green Lantern. But Wyatt had grown out of comic books as he had gotten older, especially once he joined the military.

As he pondered his path to becoming a symbol for the Brooks, he wondered how it might look in comparison to those superheroes' journeys. A secret identity was a must. As Jeff had told him, his biggest mistake in helping the man in the alley was failing to conceal his face. If Wyatt was going to bring hope to the Brooks, he needed to hide his true identity. He had to give the people a faceless hero to look up to, someone who could be anyone, anywhere, anytime.

The thought of trying to squeeze into a spandex or Lycra costume made him cringe, though. Without a properly armored suit, he was as likely to be killed on his first night out as he was to actually do any good. Anything colorful would give him away. He would stick to dark colors, street clothes. They might not protect him, but they might obscure him enough in the shadows to keep him alive.

He sketched out a few ideas. His first concept ended up making him look like a Batman-wannabe outfitted with hockey pads and a cape. *No capes.* He was bound to get tangled up in the folds of fabric. He scrapped that idea and started again. Perhaps something looser, giving him more range of movement. A hood was a decent idea, although it would need to be coupled with some kind of mask, as his encounter in the alley had proven that a hood alone was not a sufficient disguise.

That concept ended up looking like an all-black Green Arrow cosplay.

Wyatt's fingers drummed on his desk. He sat alone in the small room near the back of the house that had become his office. A stack of Ellis' comic books sat on the desk next to his notebook. Wyatt pushed past Green Lantern and Iron Man comics, briefly rifled through the pages of a Captain America story, and then stopped when his eyes fell on a vintage Daredevil comic book.

On the cover, Daredevil wore all black. His outfit was obviously not spandex, but rather a baggy sweatshirt, matching pants, and white tennis shoes. His face was concealed by a scarf wrapped around the upper half of his head. Wyatt pressed his lips together, tilted his head, and picked up his pen.

He couldn't wear a scarf. That would obscure his vision. But . . . perhaps a ski mask? The tennis shoes were out; a pair of sturdy combat boots would be more effective. A hooded jacket to shroud him in darkness would complete the ensemble.

Wyatt studied the sloppy figure he had sketched out. It halfway looked like a bank robber rather than a hero, but it was a start.

"Wyatt, baby!" Joanna called. "You'd better hurry up, or we'll be late."

He closed his notebook and stepped out of his office. Over the past several weeks, his family had attended Refuge Church's regular Sunday morning services. That night, they were also hosting a community dinner. The pastor and several members of the original Refuge Church in Lakeside were going to be there, not just visiting but serving the congregation of the West Brooks campus.

Wyatt closed the office door behind him and walked down the short hallway to the living room. The rest of the family was already waiting for him.

"Sorry about that," he said. "Time slipped away. Let's get going."

Carter, Ellis, and Rhonda filed out the front door. Joanna eased up next to Wyatt as they followed and leaned in close.

"What's got you so busy lately, baby?" she asked.

"I'll explain everything soon." He wrapped an arm around her waist and kissed her cheek. "I promise."

* * *

The fellowship hall of West Brooks Refuge Church was packed with people standing shoulder-to-shoulder. Pastor Jeff had been advertising the meal for some time as a community outreach event, with all denizens of the Brooks welcome to attend. Many members of East Brooks Refuge Church campus were there as well. Wyatt saw people he recognized from the neighborhood, those he had seen at the grocery store or the gas station or the movie theater. He was impressed by the turnout.

Silas was there, too. The tall, bald man was closer to the front of the line, carrying a baby in his left arm and standing next to his wife, who held another baby that looked just slightly older. Silas caught Wyatt's eye briefly and tilted his chin upward in greeting. Wyatt returned the greeting with a quick wave.

Carter nudged Wyatt's elbow. "Dad, do you know who that is?"

Wyatt glanced in the direction Carter was gesturing. Standing on the other side of the open kitchen window, a young man was serving from a tray of macaroni and cheese. He had light tan skin; brown eyes; and long, curly brown hair that was currently bound in a hairnet. He wore a green Henley shirt, but the quality and cut of the shirt belied its simplicity. There was no doubt it was expensive. Wyatt recognized the young man instantly.

"That's Dean Sterling," Carter continued before Wyatt could reply. "He's one of the richest dudes in Sojourn City!"

Indeed, Dean was the scion of Sterling Enterprises. He was a well-known face in the community, as he spent his wealth generously in an effort to improve the Brooks. Still, Wyatt was surprised to see him serving with the kitchen staff. His opinion of the young man rose.

As Wyatt and his family approached the front of the line, he picked up snippets of conversation coming from the kitchen. Sterling seemed intent on keeping spirits light, but a few of the others around him were downcast. A young woman with dark hair and piercing eyes that were almost black wiped a tear from her cheek. Another young man raked his fingers through blond hair and paced.

"It's been four months, Dean," the woman said. "Why can't they find him?"

Dean shoveled a pile of mac and cheese onto someone's plate and turned to her. "This is Gid we're talking about, Jolie. He's one of the toughest guys I know. If anyone can make it that long, it's him."

"We should be down there," the blond kid growled. "You've got a jet, Dean. Let's fly down and look for him ourselves. The Venezuelan authorities clearly don't care about one missing American."

Jolie put a hand on his shoulder. "The jungles are too huge, Wes. You'd end up just as lost as your brother."

"I know, but . . ."

"Let's talk about this later," Dean said. "Right now, we've got guests to serve. All we can do is keep praying that God brings Gideon home."

Wyatt wondered who they were talking about but it was none of his business. When he reached the window and held out his plate to receive his food, he intended to keep his mouth shut. But more tears welled in Jolie's eyes, and something inside Wyatt urged him to speak up. He reached across the counter and put a gentle hand on her upper arm.

"Whoever you're praying for, don't lose hope," he said. "I've seen a lot of men lost in a lot worse places find their way home."

Jolie sniffled and nodded. "Thank you."

The dinner passed cheerfully with Wyatt and Joanna letting the kids do most of the talking as they described their schoolwork, upcoming projects and events, and the latest drama with their friends. Wyatt was scraping the last of his mashed potatoes from his plate when Jeff caught his eye and gestured him over. Wyatt patted Joanna's shoulder, excused himself from the table, and weaved through the dense crowd toward the pastor.

"Good to see you, Wyatt," Jeff said. "Have you thought any more about the things we discussed?"

"I have, and—"

Jeff held up a hand. "I don't want to know. However, I did want you to have this."

He extended his hand. In it, he held a length of thin rope—twine, really. At the end of the rope dangled a wooden cross pendant about two inches long. Wyatt took the makeshift necklace from the pastor.

"What's this for?"

"A symbol." A mischievous light twinkled in Jeff's eyes. "Just thought you might need a little inspiration."

Wyatt draped the necklace over his head and tucked it under his shirt. "You know, I just might."

CHAPTER 7

Over the next few weeks, crime in the Brooks worsened. Whispers and rumors circulated that a new player was in town, a mob. Organized crime had never held a solid foothold in Sojourn City, other than the Red Dogs and Tyrants. Wyatt hardly felt they qualified as organized. If the rumors were true, the Brooks would be in more danger than ever.

A confusing upside to the increasing crime wave was that older cases took less priority. Detective Walters, the officer on the case of the man Wyatt had murdered, finally ruled that the Red Dog had been killed in a gang conflict with the Tyrants. It appeared that the cops had given up on finding the actual murderer. Wyatt was relieved that they would not be coming after him but simultaneously worried that things were so bad that a murder case could be passed over so quickly. The spirits of the Brooks' residents plummeted by the day. It was time for someone to do something.

Wyatt's strict training regimen had brought back the fighting skills he had allowed to wane over the years. Through a combination of exercises and sparring with Silas, he honed his body to become a precision instrument of damage. Even unarmed, he would be a force to be feared.

Silas, of course, did not know what he was training Wyatt for. He believed Wyatt was merely looking for an outlet to vent his frustrations, and he was happy to provide that outlet. Wyatt was glad they had met. They rarely interacted outside the gym, so Wyatt couldn't quite call Silas a friend—but . . . he was a comrade.

Wyatt dodged a left jab from the other man and retaliated with a right hook. Silas was a few inches taller than Wyatt, which made sparring with him more interesting. Wyatt did not know what kind of opposition to expect once he became this symbol, and he wanted to be ready for enemies of any size.

After trading a few more blows, Wyatt held up his gloves in a signal of surrender. Silas nodded, peeled his own gloves off, and reached for a towel.

"Doin' good, man." Silas wiped sweat from his brow and sipped from a water bottle. "If I didn't know better, I'd say you were training for the Golden Gloves."

"Something like that." Wyatt laughed. "I'm a little past my prime to be trying for that, though. I think I'll just stick to duking it out with you."

The men engaged in small talk for a few minutes as they cleaned up. Finally, Wyatt waved to Silas as he strode out the door toward his car. Somewhere in the distance, police sirens wailed. Any trace of good humor from his conversation with Silas faded, and Wyatt's lips pressed into a grim line. *I've waited long enough.* The Brooks needed its hero.

Wyatt had accumulated the pieces for his disguise gradually over the past week. He got a ski mask from a sporting goods store, a pair of tactical gloves from a surplus shop, and a black sweatshirt from a discount market. He already owned black jeans, combat boots, and a hooded black jacket. His ensemble was complete. All that remained was to hit the streets and find some crime to stop, but . . . He was afraid.

He had been lucky that the Red Dog he fought in the alley had not carried a gun. He would not be so lucky every time he fought a criminal. Wyatt was just a man, and he could be killed. It would be unspeakably embarrassing if his first effort to bring hope to the city ended with him bleeding out in a gutter somewhere.

The wooden cross from Jeff pressed against Wyatt's chest beneath his shirt.

If he did not step up, it would be someone else bleeding in that gutter. The police were stretched thin and ineffective. Someone had to fight the crime that threatened to overrun Wyatt's city. He was done pondering, done planning. It was time to take action.

He would start that night, he decided. He would have to tell Joanna, of course; but even if she resisted at first, he believed she would understand. Once she was on board, he would put on his disguise, head out onto the streets, and trust God to lead him to the crime he most needed to stop.

As Wyatt drove home, he scanned the streets. There was so much garbage piled up, so much graffiti tagging every building with an open wall. No one bothered to clean up anymore because everyone was afraid to be outside.

Ahead, a young woman sprinted around the corner, a look of dread on her face. She was blonde, maybe early twenties, dressed in a long, white trench coat. Wyatt's fingers clenched on his steering wheel. Three men rounded the corner after the woman, shouting at her. Their intention was obvious. The woman would not outrun them forever. If someone did not intervene, they would catch her and have their way.

Wyatt jerked the wheel and parked on the curb. He did not have his whole disguise with him, but his ski mask was in the glove compartment. He yanked it out, pulled it over his head, and leaped from his car. It was time for the symbol of hope to make his first appearance.

The woman had rushed into an alley in her panic. The three men were right behind her, and the leader quickly pinned her to the wall. When Wyatt had fought the Red Dog outside the grocery store, he had shouted at the man to leave his victim alone. This time, Wyatt would make no such mistake. He launched into the midst of the trio and threw a punch at the leader's jaw. His fist struck like a cannonball against a glass wall. The leader's jaw cracked beneath Wyatt's punch, and the man sagged to the ground, instantly unconscious.

While the others were frozen with confusion, Wyatt snapped out a sideways kick that caught the second man in his gut. He doubled over but did not fall. The third man scowled and brandished a switchblade. Wyatt's blood pumped. The slender knife lashed out toward him. He barely dodged aside and threw a palm strike at his opponent's chest. The man reeled back and slashed wildly. The switchblade caught Wyatt across the left bicep, a stinging bite that elicited a hiss from his lips.

The man Wyatt had kicked staggered upright, drawing in wheezing breaths. As the man with the switchblade advanced again, the second man circled to flank Wyatt. Wyatt weaved out of the way of another knife slash and drove a punch into the attacker's elbow. The joint popped, and the man cried out. Wyatt turned—

Right into a punch from the third man. Pain exploded beneath Wyatt's eye. *Broken orbital bone.* He filed the information away and retaliated with a knee strike. The man retreated against the brick wall. Wyatt grabbed his collar and slammed his back against the wall, then spun and hurled the man atop the unconscious leader. The knife-wielder was still clutching his elbow and whimpering. He backed away from Wyatt, tears welling in his eyes.

"P-please . . . don't kill us."

"Get out of here," Wyatt rumbled.

The man shuddered, nodded, and sprinted out of the alley. Wyatt glanced down at the two unconscious thugs and then turned to face the woman. She stared up at him with wide, tearful eyes. He relaxed his posture, knelt, and extended a hand to her. Her lips parted, and she let out a pitiful wail.

"Please . . . stay away . . . " She scooted closer to the wall. "Don't hurt me."

Sorrow drove like a knife blade into Wyatt's heart. He supposed in her eyes, he looked no better than her assailants. He was a broad-shouldered man in a workout tee and a ski mask, and he had just brutalized three men. Sure, those men might have been attacking her; but for all she knew, Wyatt might have just wanted her for himself. He eased away from her and held out his hands, palms-up.

"I'm not going to hurt you. I won't even touch you. I promise. I'm the good guy."

"How . . . how do I know that?" She gestured to his face. "Your mask . . . you just look like any other criminal."

"I must wear this mask to protect the ones I love. Someone has to take a stand against the evil in this city, and it's going to be me."

The woman started to rise, keeping close to the wall, but some of the fear in her eyes had started to fade. She was still tense, though. Wyatt rose as well and took a long step back to give her plenty of room.

"How will people know that?" she asked. "You're just a guy in a mask."

Wyatt supposed she was right. To become a symbol, he had to be identifiable somehow. He reached up and brushed the cross hanging beneath his shirt. Then, he drew it out and pulled it off. He tossed the necklace to the woman. She caught it and stared down at the wooden pendant.

"That's my symbol," Wyatt said. "Anyone who sees it should know that help is coming."

He turned and rushed for the street. His job was done, and he needed to get out before the unconscious thugs awoke.

"Wait!" the woman called after him. "What do we call you?"

Wyatt froze at the entrance to the alley and glanced back. That was one thing he had not considered. He had just planned on being a symbol, a nameless vigilante. He didn't think he would need a name. With no answer to give her, he turned away again and hurried out onto the street with new plans and ideas storming through his mind.

CHAPTER 8

"Are you out of your mind?"

Joanna's words didn't sting half as much as the rubbing alcohol she swabbed across the knife cut on his bicep. Wyatt hissed between his teeth as the purifying liquid brushed off the cotton swab and seeped into the wound, biting with a thousand tiny teeth. He had endured worse pain, though, so he sat still and bore it as she cleaned.

"You got away with it the first time," his wife continued. "By some miracle, you not only survived going up against a gangbanger, but you got off scot-free when you accidentally killed him. But instead of realizing that maybe there's something to be learned from all this, you go off and play hero again! You're not invincible, Wyatt. You could die."

"I know . . . I know." He ground his jaw as she came around to check the growing bruise under his eye. "But I've been thinking about this for a long time. Ever since I fought that Red Dog, actually. I did more to help that man in the alley than the police could've. I saved that young woman today from who-knows-what atrocities those men would've inflicted on her. And again, the police were nowhere to be seen. They're stretched too thin, Jo. The people of the Brooks need to be reminded that someone's watching over them."

Joanna grew quiet as she worked. She wrapped the knife wound in gauze and traced her finger gently over Wyatt's cheek. She had been a school nurse before retiring to stay home with the kids, so she knew how to handle cuts and bruises. Even so, a broken orbital bone was likely out of her wheelhouse.

"Can you move this eye?" When Wyatt demonstrated he could, she nodded. "Well, it's not that bad, then. But if the swelling doesn't go down, you're going straight to the doctor. That will need surgery." She turned to the bathroom sink, rinsed blood from her hands, and glanced back over her shoulder. "I know we need a hero, baby. I just don't understand why it has to be you. I don't want to lose you."

"I know. I don't exactly have a death wish, either."

Joanna raised an eyebrow and leaned against the edge of the sink, arms folded. "Could've fooled me."

"But I really feel like this is what I'm meant to do." Wyatt rose from where he had been sitting on the lid of the toilet. He snagged his shirt from the towel rack and slipped it on. "I need your support on this, Jo. I won't do it if you're not on board. But I just know that the right hero and the right symbol are exactly what this city needs to turn things around. If I can't be that hero, at least I can be the one who inspires the next one."

Joanna rested her hands on the bowl of the sink and stared down into the basin. Wyatt came up behind her and wrapped his arms around her waist. If only she understood that he was doing this for her and the kids more than anyone else. They deserved to live in a city where it was safe to play in the streets, to walk to school, to enjoy a day in the park without fear of some gangster shooting them up.

"Normally, I'll only do this at night," he said. "I'll stick to the shadows. If I do it right, most of the guys I fight won't ever see me coming."

Her head came up, and she made eye contact with Wyatt through the mirror. "And if they do?"

"If they do . . . I'll just trust God to take care of me."

"You're really serious about this, aren't you?"

Wyatt chopped his head in a single nod. "Serious as a bomb threat."

"Okay." Joanna trembled, took a shaky breath, and turned to face him. Her hands rested gently on his chest. "Then you be the best vigilante you can be. Train until you can't see straight anymore, until your whole body is a weapon. Use the shadows and the reputation you'll build to make every criminal in this city so scared of you that they won't even think about fighting back. Become something too terrifying to fight."

"I will. I promise."

"Good. Because I can't keep fixing you up like this. I'll have to start billing you."

Wyatt laughed. "Whatever the cost, I'll pay it. I could use your help with something else, though. That girl in the alley—she was scared of me, too. I don't want the innocent to fear me. I need to incorporate a cross symbol into what I do somehow, so victims and criminals alike recognize me. And I'll need a name."

Joanna picked up the ski mask Wyatt had laid on the counter. "Give me a few minutes with a needle and thread, and I can come up with something. I don't know about a name, though. You'll have to ask someone else for help with that."

* * *

Wyatt ultimately decided that his children deserved to know what he was doing, too. He could not avoid them, and they would see him coming home at night with cuts and bruises. Rather than let them worry that he was being beaten up needlessly, he and Joanna agreed that they should know that he was fighting for a safer city. He gathered them in the living room, sat all three on the couch, and explained his plan.

Even as pre-teens, Ellis and Rhonda understood. They seemed scared, but Wyatt assured them that he would be all right, that he could take care of himself. They nodded soberly and hugged him.

Carter was a different story, one entirely more worrisome. He thought what Wyatt was doing was cool. Wyatt warned him that his actions were not about being cool. The life he was about to lead was serious, potentially deadly, and he did not approach it lightly. Even so, Carter approved unequivocally.

"It's about time someone did something," the boy said. "Those punk Red Dogs and Tyrants need to know they don't own this part of town."

Wyatt clenched his jaw. "You're right. Just don't get any ideas. This is my burden to bear, understand? You don't tell anyone about this, and you don't do anything to try to help me. It's my mission, not yours."

"What are you going to call yourself?" Ellis asked.

"I'm still trying to figure that part out. I know I need a name, one the criminals will fear and the innocents of the Brooks will look to for hope, but . . . I don't know what that name is. All I know is, I'm using a cross as my symbol."

"A cross?" Rhonda cupped her chin in one hand. "How about 'the Crusader?' They wore crosses on their armor and shields. And they did a lot of really bad things, but . . . maybe you can take that name and make it mean something good, instead?"

Wyatt exchanged glances with Joanna. *The Crusader.* It sounded perfect to him. It was simple, a descriptor more than a name, but it fit.

It was another way of calling him "the vigilante," but it meant more. A crusade implied a mission, a goal. Anyone could take the law into their own hands and be a vigilante. A grieving father, a protective mother . . . anyone with a gun and someone who had wronged them could be a vigilante. But a crusader? That was more.

It was Wyatt.

"Thank you, Rho." Wyatt reached down and brushed her cheek. "That's exactly who I'm going to be."

CHAPTER 9

The following day, Wyatt felt an odd mixture of dread and excitement as he went to work. That night, he would make his official debut as the Crusader. He did not know where or how yet, but he knew it had to be that night. The sooner the people of the Brooks saw someone fighting for them, the better.

All day, as he worked the assembly line next to his friend Lionel, he imagined different scenarios playing out. Would he catch a random mugger in the act? Perhaps it would be a gang of robbers knocking off a convenience store. Or maybe it would be official gang activity by the Red Dogs or Tyrants. Whomever he faced, he would make an example of them and leave them terrified of the shadows.

"You good, Wyatt?" Lionel quirked an eyebrow. "You're moving a little slow today."

Lionel was a burly man with dark brown skin, a thick beard, and a buzz cut. He was as strong as they came; he even had some mass on Wyatt, which came from years of brute force exertion and lifting near-impossible weights on the pharmaceutical packing line. Many lines like the ones Wyatt and Lionel manned were automated. Not in the Brooks. Though other parts of Sojourn City were outfitted with bleeding edge tech, the Brooks was the last in line for that sort of thing. There, the strength of a worker's back was the only technology that mattered.

Wyatt refocused his attention on the work at hand. "Sorry, man. I've just got some stuff on my mind, is all."

"Who doesn't? Hey, would you mind if I bum a ride home with you tonight? My car's on the fritz again, and I had to get a rideshare just to get here today. That pretty much drained my disposable income, so I can't afford to get one back; and I really don't feel like walking across the Brooks so close to dark."

Wyatt knew his own family struggled financially, but Lionel was even worse off. He liked to help the guy out when he could—especially since Lionel had gotten Wyatt the job at the factory in the first place. Lionel was rough around the edges, a guy who had grown up on the streets and never quite been able to escape them. But he tried, and that was more than Wyatt could say for some of the characters he had seen in the Brooks. For that alone, Lionel deserved the investment of time and friendship. Wyatt hoped he could be a good influence on the man and eventually help him, as Lionel had helped Wyatt.

"You got it," he said.

"Thanks, Wyatt. You're a pal."

The day passed slowly, as was typical of any work day when Wyatt was looking forward to something at the end of it. Sometimes, the monotony of working a loading job allowed him to fall into a rhythm that made time pass in a blur. His thoughts could wander as his hands worked, and he would look up to find that hours had passed in a blink. But that day, with his thoughts so focused on getting to the end of his shift, each tick of the clock's hand dragged into eons.

It was nearing time for the lunch break when Wyatt excused himself from the line to go to the restroom. He faced his reflection in the bathroom mirror and stared himself down. *Get your head in the game, Wyatt.*

Becoming the Crusader was a daunting and exciting prospect, but it was only a facet of his life. He still had responsibilities to his family, which included doing his job well enough to keep on the boss' good side. Layoffs were not uncommon in facilities like the one Wyatt worked at, especially in such a financially difficult time. The last thing he needed was to get cut from the workforce because his focus was off.

The whistle blew, signaling the beginning of lunch hour. Wyatt washed his hands and stepped out of the bathroom. By the time he made it back to the assembly line floor, most of the other workers were gone. Lionel was still at their station, so Wyatt weaved his way toward his friend. He opened his mouth to call Lionel to lunch.

He stopped when he saw Lionel stuffing several packages from the assembly line into his backpack. Lionel looked up, saw Wyatt, and froze with wide-eyed shock. Wyatt clenched his fists and stormed toward his friend. As he did, he looked around to make sure no one else was in the area, especially a supervisor.

"Are you out of your mind?" he demanded. "What are you doing?"

"Do you know what these pills go for?" Lionel resumed stuffing his backpack. "I know a guy in the far west part of the Brooks who'll pay top dollar."

"And he won't wonder where you got them?"

"Don't ask; don't tell."

Wyatt grabbed his friend's wrist. "Lionel, you can't do this. Forget that it's wrong in the first place—if you get caught, you won't just get fired. They'll call the cops in a second!"

"I need the cash. Gotta take the risk."

"This isn't the way."

They froze, staring at each other. Lionel tried to pull away from Wyatt, but Wyatt tightened his grip. Lionel looked down at Wyatt's hand in bewilderment and then back up at his face, shaking his head.

"You don't gotta be such a boy scout, man. You really think this'll hurt the company? I'm just doing what's necessary to keep my head above water."

"You're better than this, Lionel. Put it back."

Lionel's jaws locked, and his dark eyes filled with fury. For a moment, Wyatt thought his friend would take a swing and run off with his prize. But finally, Lionel huffed and pulled the packages of pills out of his bag.

"I know you're right, man. It's just hard to resist when the old bank account's looking so close to empty."

Wyatt released his hold on Lionel. "Believe me, I understand. You're doing the right thing, though. Just hang in there. You'll make it through. One day, the Brooks will start to get better."

"Yeah? Will we get visits from Santa and see unicorns prancing down the streets, too?" Lionel hung his head and shook it. "Face it, man. The only way the Brooks will get any better is if the one-percenters up on the Platform decide to pour money our way. And you and I both know that's never gonna happen. Life here's not gonna change unless it's by our own hands."

Wyatt resisted the urge to chuckle. Lionel had no idea how right he was. If it was up to Wyatt and his hands, things would be very different before long.

CHAPTER 10

Standing on a rooftop overlooking the intersection of Washington and Eighth Streets in the Brooks, Wyatt worked to steady his trembling hands. It had been a challenge just to clamber onto the roof, but it felt right to start his crusading career that way. That was where all the notable comic book heroes went to watch over their cities; and though Wyatt intended to be more serious than a comic book character, he acknowledged the need to play into that kind of mythology to build his reputation.

The trouble was, he had no idea if any criminal activity would happen on that particular block. He had selected it at random, mostly because Washington almost completely bisected the Brooks from north to south. It was not a perfect split, as Washington diverted west when it reached the canal that split the Brooks from east to west; but it was still a pulsing artery that connected most of the activity in the neighborhood. If something was going to happen, it would be somewhere along the avenue.

Do I need a voice in my ear? Though Wyatt had given up his superhero reading at a much younger age, he had watched some of the TV shows and movies that Ellis enjoyed. Almost all of the superheroes had a comrade who remained at the home base in radio contact with the hero. That person would alert the hero to police reports or camera footage of crimes in progress. Wyatt imagined that with someone like that on his side, being the Crusader would be a lot easier.

Unfortunately, he did not know anyone with access to a police radio, nor anyone with the computer skills necessary to capture CCTV footage. He would have to play things by his own ear, reacting only to situations near enough to his current position. He would miss a lot of crime; but over weeks and months, he would build his reputation. Perhaps he would even build a team. Someone with the skills Wyatt needed might reach out to the Crusader once his reputation was established.

Ideally, Wyatt would have liked to have a stable enough relationship with the police that they would at least leave him alone to pursue his own activity. He was doing their job, after all. But he expected that for the first few months at least, the police would see him as another threat. He could only hope that they prioritized catching murderers, traffickers, and drug dealers over a masked man trying to help.

"God . . ." Wyatt spoke softly, though no one was around to overhear. "I'm Your soldier. Point me in the right direction."

He stood there for a long time, his eyes drifting across the surrounding area and the distant lights of the skyscrapers in Lakeside on the horizon. This was his city, his home. He was ready to reclaim it.

He flexed his fingers sheathed in tactical gloves and rolled his shoulders. He wondered if he had made the right wardrobe choices. It was spring, and summer was on its way. A black leather jacket and other dark, heavy garb would be especially uncomfortable on those hot summer nights. Still, he needed all the disguise he could get. If he remained anonymous and—to criminals—terrifying, he would bear the discomfort.

Bang. Bang.

Wyatt's blood ran cold at the echoing gunshots. He swiveled his head around, searching for the source. It sounded like it had come from his left; and judging by the reverberation of the echo, it had probably been in an alley. *Typical.* So far, all his fights had been in alleys. Wyatt pulled on his ski mask, which Joanna had stitched with a silver cross on the forehead, and dropped down to the fire escape. He mounted the ladder and descended it. At the bottom, he took off out into the streets and hurried north.

He peered down each alley as he ran. Each one was empty, save for the occasional vagabond wrapped in tattered garments and huddling near dumpsters. He hoped he had gone the right direction and that the echo had not thrown him off the trail. If so, he would never find the shooter. *It might already be too late.* It wasn't often that gunshots went off that the target remained alive more than a few minutes after, especially in an alley.

Someone screamed nearby. Wyatt picked up the pace and rounded the corner into the next alley. He found a young couple backing into a corner. Four men surrounded them. The apparent leader brandished a gun, while the others were armed with a baseball bat, a length of chain, and a long combat knife. The young man clutched his lower abdomen, and blood seeped from between his fingers. He stood between the assailants and the young woman, his face ashen, but his eyes full of defiance.

"I'm impressed." The gang leader twirled his gun. "It's not many folks that are brave enough to stand up to the Tyrants. Even less who keep standing after we've put a hole in 'em. Now, I wager you've got a few more minutes to live. Give us your stuff, and you can call the authorities. Maybe an ambulance will get here in time to save your life. Maybe not."

The man with the baseball bat snickered. "Not likely out here, boss."

"Not especially, no. But if you refuse us, you'll spend your last few minutes watching us take your girl. Your choice."

Wyatt clenched his fist. *Here goes nothing.* He dropped into the shadows of the alley and scooped a crowbar from the ground near the dumpster. As he approached unseen, he scraped the metal bar across the brick wall. The harsh scratching brought the Tyrants to a halt, and the man with the gun whirled around. Wyatt eased back into the cover of darkness.

"What was that?" the man with the knife demanded.

"Probably nothin'," Baseball Bat replied. "Let's focus and get the job done."

Earlier in the evening, Wyatt had filled his pocket with an assortment of pebbles and loose bolts and screws. He reached into the pocket and took one of them between his fingers, flicking it down into the alley where it skipped across the pavement and splashed into a low puddle. The Tyrants whirled again, searching for the source of the noise.

"Something funny's going on," the gunman growled.

It was time to act. If Wyatt did not hurry, the young man was going to bleed out. *God, help me.*

He leaped and used a fire escape ladder as a fulcrum to vault from. His booted feet came down directly on the Tyrant's back. The thug grunted and canted forward, dropping his knife. Wyatt spun and punched the chain-wielder across the jaw and again in the ribs. As the Tyrant folded, Wyatt shoved him back into the gunman.

Bang. The shot went high and struck the alley wall above Wyatt's head. He surged forward to attack his last foe, the man with the baseball bat. The Tyrant swung wildly. Wyatt ducked underneath and punched the thug in the elbow. Something popped, but the Tyrant merely released the bat and lunged at Wyatt with a blood curdling howl.

Wyatt shielded his face with his forearms as blows rained down from the Tyrant's meaty fists. He hooked his booted foot behind one of the Tyrant's legs and bucked his hips. The Tyrant went flying off Wyatt to land on top of the staggering knife-wielder. As Wyatt clambered to his feet, the guy with the chain lashed out. The links caught Wyatt across the arm with a stinging bite, a blow that he knew would leave a distinctive bruise. He clenched his jaw and pressed in as the chain came back around to strike his left shoulder. Wyatt brought his knee up into the man's groin and then pummeled him across the cheek and square in the nose.

The gunman was finally staggering to his feet, and he brought his gun to bear on Wyatt. Wyatt tucked into a roll and snagged the chain from the limp fingers of its wielder. The shooter opened fire, but Wyatt's role carried him out of the man's line of sight. As he came up in a crouch, Wyatt lashed out with the chain, striking the gunman's hand. The gun clattered to the alley floor as Wyatt leapt atop the leader of the gang and showered him with punches and elbow strikes.

Finally, the attackers stopped moving.

The young woman wailed in the corner, shouting into her phone for help. Wyatt stepped over the unconscious thugs and knelt next to her companion. He was still alive; but his pallor had worsened, and his breathing was shallow. Wyatt pulled a wadded-up handkerchief from his pocket and stuffed it against the bullet wound. The woman looked up tearfully at Wyatt and lowered her phone.

"Th-thank you . . . "

"You're welcome. Is help coming?"

She nodded. "The ambulance is on the way."

"Good. Keep pressure on his wound until they get here. Containing the bleeding is the most important thing to ensure his survival."

"O-okay. Who . . . who are you?"

Wyatt rose from his kneeling position and turned to face the Tyrants. They were stirring, but none rose to challenge him. He grabbed the knife-wielder by the collar and hoisted him to his feet. Then, he spoke loudly enough for the woman and her friend to hear, though his eyes were locked on those of the Tyrant.

"I'm the Crusader," he announced. "Spread the word. The Brooks are under my protection. Any trouble gets stirred up, I'll be there to stop it. I'm in the shadows, always watching, always protecting. You want to go tear up the other gangs? That's your business. But you leave the innocent people of this city alone. If you don't, I'll come back for you. And next time, I'll use the crowbar."

He shoved the knife-wielder away. The man squealed and sprinted out of the alley. Wyatt stepped over each of the remaining gangsters and zip-tied their hands and feet together. In the distance, sirens wailed; but they were ambulance sirens. That was good for the gunshot victim, but the police were still needed. Wyatt knelt to scoop up the gunman's weapon. Then, he aimed it at the sky and squeezed the trigger until the magazine was empty. That amount of gunfire would surely draw attention. The young woman yelped, pressed herself closer to the injured man, and stared up at the Crusader.

"You're really here to help us?" she asked.

He nodded. "I am. The Brooks have suffered long enough. From now on, I'm going to fight back. If the gangs want to take over this city, they'll have to climb over the pile of their injured buddies I'll make as they send 'em my way. No one terrorizes this city on my watch." Wyatt scaled up the fire escape to watch until help arrived. "Not anymore."

CHAPTER 11

The following nights stretched into weeks, and the weeks stretched into months. Slowly but surely, the Crusader's reputation grew. At first, no one seemed to take him seriously. Some claimed he was an urban legend, while others—those who had encountered him—insisted he was real, but he was just a simple man, a man who could be killed. Every night, Wyatt disproved that concept by surviving unlikely odds.

He did not survive unscathed, though. He came home so regularly with bruises, cuts, and contusions that Joanna had taken to leaving the first aid kit out on the counter so she could tend to him as soon as he arrived.

"I'm going to start charging you a nursing fee," she warned.

Wyatt laughed at that. "You know I can't afford it. You've seen our finances."

Something Wyatt had not taken into consideration was that his work as the Crusader would have an effect on his job. His work at the factory was intense, and there were days when he struggled to keep up with the assembly line. He did his best to hide it, hoping that his supervisor would not notice. Without much time to sleep, it was getting harder.

Eventually, the gangs seemed to realize that the Crusader was a real threat that was not going away. Crime numbers dipped infinitesimally but then surged again as the gangs solved their problem by going out in greater numbers. Wyatt had been lucky to take on four at a time when he took them by surprise. Groups of five or more would be nearly impossible for him to handle alone.

He could not quit, though. He continued to do his best, tackling the smaller groups when he could and relying on his growing reputation to intimidate those he faced. Sometimes, a gang of five or seven would dwindle to three or four by the time the Crusader emerged from the shadows because he used stealth and brutality to frighten them. Although he was just a man, the gangs had seen what he did to the criminals he got his hands on. Their fear made him more than a man in their eyes. He was a presence, an ever-lurking phantom to be feared. Any scrape or clank in an alley could be the Crusader lurking in wait. That turned the tide enough for him to claim victory, although he usually came out of those fights worse for wear.

The police seemed irritated by his presence, but they were too focused on the gangs to commit to chasing a vigilante. That was a relief, though Wyatt wished they would leave him alone altogether or, better yet, side with him. If they realized the good he was doing and that he could help them, the cleanup of the Brooks would go that much faster.

Before long, the Crusader became the talk of the neighborhood. Wyatt's coworkers talked of him in hushed tones during their shift and argued about him on their lunch break. Some believed he was making a difference. Others worried he would only make the gangs—and an expanding mafia spoken of only in whispers—angrier. At church, Wyatt heard parishioners speculating about why the city's new hero had co-opted the cross as his symbol. A few of them considered it blasphemy, but the majority thought he was merely trying to show that he stood for good.

Pastor Jeff never confronted Wyatt about the Crusader, never even hinted that he knew they were one and the same. He had to know, given their past conversations and the wooden cross Jeff had given him. Still, the conversation Wyatt expected to come never did. It seemed the pastor was content to let Wyatt keep his secret.

It was a miracle word had not gotten out through Wyatt's kids. They told him almost every night that their classmates raved about the Crusader. Some had taken to stitching crosses on their clothes in solidarity with the vigilante. The school board was split on how to handle the situation, as by taking the law into his own hands the Crusader was technically a criminal; but they saw the boost his presence had on student morale. Still, Wyatt expected Crusader adornments to be banned in the coming weeks.

"They can't ban a cross, Dad," Carter argued at the dinner table one evening. "It's a symbol of faith. They can't even specify silver crosses because lots of kids wear silver necklaces with a cross pendant. If they try to ban it, the Christian parents will get up in arms; and then it'll turn into a big mess."

Wyatt lowered his head to conceal a smile. "Well, whatever happens, I'm just glad to know my mission is working."

He doubted he would ever rid the Brooks of gang activity altogether. But as long as he was bringing hope and inspiring the people around him, he was accomplishing his goal. That was something that couldn't be taken from him.

After dinner, he took the dishes to the sink and rinsed them off. On the nights when he did not go out as the Crusader, he tried to do extra chores and be especially present with the family to make up for the nights he was gone. He could not replace time lost, but he could use the time he had effectively.

"Hey, Dad!" Ellis's prepubescent voice cracked fearfully from the living room. "You're gonna wanna see this."

Wyatt frowned, set the plate he was holding on the drying rack, and stepped out of the kitchen. The family was gathered around the TV, which was turned to a local news station. A helicopter's view showed a gas station surrounded by police cars with sirens flashing. The text at the bottom of the screen read, *Red Dogs take hostages, demand surrender of the Crusader.*

Wyatt's blood ran cold. "Turn it up."

"The hostage situation escalated this evening as the gang members barricaded themselves inside the gas station," the anchorwoman said. "Police confirm that there are at least five hostages inside, and all efforts to negotiate have failed. Sources tell us that the Red Dogs are refusing to speak to anyone except the Crusader, who they are demanding surrender himself to them immediately."

Carter turned to him. "What are you going to do?"

Wyatt stood rooted in place for a long moment, staring at the screen. *I never meant for it to come to this.* The Crusader was supposed to protect the innocent, not be the reason they were endangered. But of course, the gang had realized that the Crusader had one weakness they could exploit: the people he had vowed to watch over. He would not stand for it.

"I'm going to go there." Wyatt saw the fear on Joanna's face and the pride on Carter's. He saw the concern in the way Ellis and Rhonda huddled together. He knew they worried for him, but he had a job to do. "I'm going to stop them. And I'm going to make sure they never try something like this again."

CHAPTER 12

Sneaking up to the gas station was no easy feat. The police had the block cordoned off, and they would not just let Wyatt walk through the barricade. In fact, if the Crusader showed his face, Wyatt suspected he would be quickly arrested. The police could not ignore him anymore. His existence had caused peril for innocent civilians. The cops would be forced to acknowledge that and react.

To avoid a scene, Wyatt climbed onto a rooftop a full block from the gas station and moved down the street from rooftop to rooftop. Jumping some of the gaps was difficult, but he had learned to navigate the treacherous terrain over the past several months of activity. It only took him five minutes to traverse the block and kneel unseen on the building just behind the gas station. From that position, he overlooked a compact, square loading space connected to the road by a narrow alley. A freight truck rested with its trailer backed up to the gas station, and a series of pallets were stacked next to a dumpster on the opposite side of the truck.

There was a guard—a Red Dog armed with a shotgun—posted outside the rear door. The Crusader would have to take him out first. Wyatt descended a ladder onto the second-story fire escape. From there, he bounded atop the freight truck's trailer. He landed with a forward roll, hoping to minimize the noise of the impact. He immediately flattened himself atop the trailer and glanced over the edge. The Red Dog had not shifted from his position and looked unconcerned. Satisfied that he remained undetected, Wyatt eased from the trailer to the top of the dumpster, used the pallets as steps down to the ground, and rounded the front of the freight truck.

The trick would be to approach the guard unseen. But the shadows were his ally, and he had a reputation to maintain. There would be no scraping or pebble-throwing this time. The Crusader had to be a ghost, a whisper. If the thugs inside got wind that he was coming, the hostages were doomed.

His booted feet padded softly on the concrete. He crept forward with immaculate care. When he was two steps from the Red Dog, he lunged. He took the guard in a chokehold from behind, pressing the crook of his elbow into the man's windpipe. With his other hand, he twisted the shotgun aside. Then, he hooked his arm upward and used it as leverage to keep his hold on the Red Dog. The thug tried to wriggle free, but the Crusader kicked the back of his knee, throwing his leg out and stealing his leverage. Finally, the Red Dog slumped forward. Wyatt zip-tied his hands and tossed him on top of the pallets. Then, he emptied the shotgun of its shells and tossed the weapon into a pile of garbage bags.

Slowly, silently, he opened the door. The gas station's rear stock room was dark and silent. The Crusader eased inside and closed the door behind him. He hurried behind the cover of a shelving unit and peered out. Two Red Dogs patrolled the stock room, and he spied at least one more gangster through the open door to the front of the store.

To get there, Wyatt would have to take out both guards in the back silently. If the man in the front noticed, odds were good he would open fire on the hostages.

Here goes nothing.

As the closer of the two guards passed, the Crusader fell in line next to him, pacing him on the other side of the shelves. When the Red Dog reached the end of the unit, the Crusader leaped out, covered the Red Dog's mouth with one hand, and tugged him back into the shadows. A quick chin strike left the man unconscious. Wyatt bound him and tucked him away in the shadows.

One down, one to go.

He circled around the room toward the other patrolling guard. It would only be a matter of seconds until he noticed the first guard was missing. The Crusader launched himself from cover as the guard neared, turning his jump into a blow as he brought his knee up to crack across the Red Dog's chin. The guard crumpled. Wyatt caught him and dragged him, too, into the shadows.

With the back clear, he crept closer to the door to get a better look at the front of the store. The gas station was lit only by the flashing blue police lights outside. The closest guard to Wyatt remained still with his back turned. By the lights, Wyatt counted three additional Red Dogs. He could not see the hostages; they must have been hidden down one of the aisles.

Wyatt grabbed a wooden broom as he neared the front of the store. With a quick twist, he removed the broom head, leaving behind a crude but effective staff. Keeping the improvised weapon close, the Crusader approached the Red Dog blocking him from the rest of the building. As quietly as he could manage, Wyatt snaked the broomstick around the gangster's neck and tugged him backward. The Red Dog let out a choking gulp but remained otherwise silent. Wyatt dragged him into the back room, spun him around, and slammed his head twice into the wall.

As the guard fell, his rifle clattered to the ground. The Crusader cringed and ducked back into the shadows. Footsteps thumped against the linoleum convenience store floor. A Red Dog stuck his head into the back room.

"Chuck? Vinnie? Devil Dan?" The gangster whispered a shaky oath. "Someone's here. Look alert, guys! It's gotta be him!"

"How do you know?" one of the others replied.

"Who else could take out our boys silently? I swear, the Crusader's a ghost."

The gangster rushed back into the front of the store. Wyatt stepped around the body of his latest victim. It seemed he remained unseen, but the gangsters knew he was there somewhere, given the absence of their comrades. The Crusader could use that knowledge to his advantage. The Red Dogs would be spooked, jittery. That fear was a greater weapon than any improvised tool the Crusader could pick up.

He rounded the corner into the front of the store and hefted his broomstick staff. One Red Dog stood directly ahead, down one of the aisles, his back to the Crusader and his head swinging back and forth as he cradled a pistol. The Crusader charged him, slamming into him from behind and sending him sailing into the refrigerators along the back wall. The glass door that took the brunt of the impact shattered, and soda bottles and sports drink cans clattered to the floor. Many of them exploded as the bottled-up carbonation detonated, sending them spiraling across the store. The Crusader drove his booted foot into the Red Dog's head for good measure, then quickly retreated down the aisle he had emerged from.

Crouching in the cover of a dark corner, Wyatt watched as the two remaining Red Dogs hurried to their fallen comrade.

"What just happened?" one exclaimed.

"It's that vigilante." The other hefted his weapon, an AK-47. "He's tryin' to scare us, but he's just one man. Not no ghost. Stick with me. We'll take him down."

They started down an aisle parallel to the one the Crusader occupied. Once they were out of sight, Wyatt surged forward, pacing them on his side of the shelves. Taking on both of them would be a challenge . . . unless he didn't have to. He waited until they were both in the middle of the aisle. Then, gathering himself, he charged—and slammed with the full force of his body into the shelves.

The shelves went down, tipping over toward the two gangsters. One of them cried out, and a gunshot cracked. Glass rained down from above as the bullet struck an unlit fluorescent light. The shelf Wyatt struck had careened down on top of the Red Dogs, pinning them to the floor. One, further ahead than his comrade, managed to clamber out from underneath; and he reached for his AK-47. The Crusader leaped onto him, striking his jaw with the edge of his staff and then kicking him in the gut to spin him over. As the Red Dog tumbled, the Crusader continued his advance. The Red Dog gasped in a breath and whipped a switchblade from his pocket. The Crusader knocked the weapon aside with his staff and jammed the end of the wooden rod into the man's solar plexus. Wildly, the Red Dog threw a punch. The blow missed the Crusader but succeeded in snapping his broomstick in half. The Crusader tossed aside the remnants and surged in, plowing his fist into the Red Dog's nose. Finally, the gangster crumpled and lay still.

"Up here!" someone called. "Help!"

Wyatt rushed to the front of the store. The hostages were lined up in front of the store's windows, kneeling with their hands resting on their heads. They were human shields, Wyatt realized—kept in place to prevent the police from firing into the store. Wyatt put his hand on the shoulder of the nearest hostage.

"You're safe," he said. "The Red Dogs are taken care of."

The hostage, a middle-aged man with thinning hair, sagged. "Oh, thank you. Thank you!"

Wyatt backed away as the hostages rose. He saw movement outside—police rushing for the door. *That's my cue to exit.*

As the hostages lauded him with thanks, he rushed back through the stock room and for the back door. Some of the Red Dogs he had knocked out earlier were conscious again, thrashing against their zip ties and shouting at him. He ignored them. Behind him, he heard the front door crash open.

"Police!" someone shouted. "Everyone stay still!"

Wyatt spared a quick glance over his shoulder as he pressed through the back door. The cops had swarmed in and were surrounding the unconscious Red Dogs, while a young woman in an officer's uniform escorted the hostages outside. It was difficult to tell from that distance, but Wyatt thought she looked familiar.

Paying it no further mind, he stepped out into the rear loading area—and stopped in his tracks as two men in leather jackets moved to block his path. Each man was disguised with a bandana around the lower half of his face. One carried a short, jagged machete; and the other brandished a pair of collapsible batons.

"Well, well." The man with the machete pointed his weapon at Wyatt. "Looks like our target came right to us, Scrap."

"Lucky for us, Plunge." The other man twirled his batons and narrowed his eyes. "Saves us the trouble of hunting him down."

CHAPTER 13

The Crusader lunged aside as the two mysterious men attacked. Given their armaments and their statements, he suspected they were either high-profile Red Dogs, better trained than their comrades, or bounty hunters hired by the Red Dogs to kill him. In fact, they had probably been the true trap all along. No matter. Red Dogs, bounty hunters . . . Wyatt would take down anyone who tried to face him.

As he rolled aside, he spotted the shotgun he had earlier tossed aside, partially hidden beneath the haphazard pile of trash bags. He scooped up the shotgun and threw it at Scrap. The glorified thug stumbled back as the weapon clattered into him, knocking one of his batons free of his grip. The Crusader tucked into a forward roll, scooped the baton from the ground, and used it to strike the back of Scrap's knee. He continued into another somersault and came up in a ready crouch on the other side of the loading space.

"Not bad." Plunge chuckled. "Good. We prefer a challenge."

Plunge charged. He swept his sword in from the right. The Crusader blocked with the baton and backed away to raise a second block as Plunge came in from the left, instead. As Plunge overstepped, the Crusader rushed at him and aimed a strike beneath the mercenary's armpit. Plunge turned and took the strike on the bicep, grimaced, and launched an overhand strike. The Crusader sidestepped it and struck

Plunge across the jaw. A distinct *crack* sounded as the truncheon met bone. As Plunge staggered, the Crusader hooked his truncheon behind the man's neck, yanked him forward, and drove his knee upward into Plunge's gut.

Scrap's pounding footsteps drew the Crusader's attention; and he turned just in time to avoid the man's swinging baton, a blow that would have flayed open Wyatt's cheek. The combatants exchanged a series of baton strikes, landing glancing blows or catching the other's weapon on the shaft of their own. Finally, the Crusader struck Scrap's face. He knelt and took out the man's knee from behind. Scrap fell, and the Crusader delivered an elbow strike to the bounty hunter's jaw. Scrap went still.

A stinging bite opened across the Crusader's bicep. Wyatt hissed and staggered back, clutching the wound. Blood seeped between the fingers of his tactical glove. Plunge snarled and lunged in. The Crusader barely avoided the next slash—and the next.

Teach me to let my guard down.

Plunge advanced viciously, his blade pushing Wyatt back toward the corner of the loading space. The bounty hunter was trying to pin him in, leaving him with no escape.

Not gonna happen.

As Plunge's next swing passed, the Crusader leaped and spun mid-air into an overhead kick. His boot contacted Plunge's weapon hand, and the machete clattered to the ground. Wyatt landed on both feet and, as Plunge turned to reach for his sword, snaked out a right hook. The punch clacked Plunge's teeth together, and the bounty hunter sank to the ground next to Scrap. Wyatt stood over them, his chest heaving as he panted for breath. It came in thick and wet through his ski mask, so he tugged it halfway up to the bridge of his nose and inhaled deep breaths of cool air.

He dropped Scrap's baton onto the ground next to the unconscious men. That would teach the Red Dogs to send anyone after him—and it would only serve to further the Crusader's reputation. Even a duo of professional mercenaries couldn't drop him.

The convenience store's back door squeaked open. Wyatt turned and rushed up the pallets, which he used to climb back atop the freight truck's trailer. From there, he watched as two cops hurried into the loading area. One was an older man with a dark skin tone, and the other was the same young woman from inside. She knelt next to the bodies and pulled their bandanas free.

"Who are they, Jolie?" the man asked.

She shook her head. "Not sure. They're alive, though."

"Think the Crusader did this?"

"Before tonight, I would've said the Crusader was an urban legend." Jolie stood and took a pair of handcuffs from her belt. "Now, I don't see how we can deny he's real. But he could be more trouble than he's worth, Paul."

"Well, maybe . . ."

"Let's get these guys cuffed up and in a squad car," Jolie said. "I'm already furious that I missed Gideon's homecoming because of the Red Dogs."

Wyatt remained on top of the truck until Paul and Jolie woke the bounty hunters and dragged them back through the store. Once he was alone, he put his mask back on, climbed to the rooftop, and headed for home. He had wounds that Joanna would need to bandage, but that did not prevent a wider smile from spreading across his face.

Maybe not all the police thought he was a help, but some did—and more importantly, all the hostages did, too. And the Red Dogs knew more than ever that he was not someone to be trifled with.

Whatever trouble came next for the Brooks, its people would know that the Crusader was there to watch their backs.

CHAPTER 14

Six months later

Though the Crusader's reputation grew, other areas in Wyatt's life were not so good. Lionel was caught stealing at the warehouse and was promptly fired. Wyatt maintained contact with his friend, encouraging Lionel to find a new job—and be more honest about it—but Lionel remained sullen and feared he would not be able to afford his apartment for much longer unless extreme steps were taken.

Wyatt invited Lionel to his house often, hoping to uplift him and be a good example. Over the following weeks, Lionel grew closer—not just with Wyatt but with the rest of the family. He had been a longtime friend, anyway; but the more time they spent together, the more Wyatt's kids grew to like Lionel. They even took to referring to him as "Uncle Lionel" on occasion. Wyatt was glad they were bonding, but he hoped that they did not take his bad example to heart. He did not need his sons or daughter stealing from their workplaces.

Wyatt tried to convince Lionel to come to church with them, but Lionel repeatedly refused. He was uninterested in any kind of religion. All he cared about was finding his next paycheck.

Unfortunately, Wyatt's own fortunes took a turn for the worse shortly after. The warehouse was forced into layoffs, and Wyatt was one of the unfortunate souls terminated. He was as jobless as Lionel.

If Wyatt did not find something soon, his family would be on the streets—which was where Wyatt found himself one chilly afternoon, standing next to a trash can fire with Lionel.

They had taken to frequenting the corners, hoping someone would drive by in need of extra hands for a construction project or manual labor. That kind of work was difficult to come across in the Brooks, but it was all Wyatt had until one of the work applications he had put out brought him results.

"Hey." Lionel nudged Wyatt's shoulder. "Look at that. Can you believe it? The nerve to drive that thing in this neighborhood . . . "

Wyatt followed Lionel's gaze. A new-model navy blue sports car pulled into a parking lot nearby. The driver turned off the engine and stepped out, revealing a light-skinned young man with blond hair and a neatly-trimmed beard. He wore a bomber jacket the same color as his car; and the quality of his jeans and boots, combined with his car, indicated that he was far better off than most of the Brooks' residents.

The man walked in their direction. Lionel scooped a scrap of newspaper off the ground, tossed it into the fire, and leaned in close to Wyatt.

"Let's see if we can't get some sympathy," he said. "This looks like the kind of guy who might like to give handouts to make himself feel better about his own wallet."

Wyatt shook his head. "Lionel . . . "

As the young man came closer, Wyatt thought he recognized him. He was definitely from the church. In fact, that was probably where he was going. Wyatt and Lionel were just down the block from the church. As the man made eye contact with Wyatt, a glint of recognition passed through his blue eyes. *Oh.* Wyatt remembered his name with a start—Gideon Turner. He was the son of the Lakeside Refuge Church's pastor, the one who had gone missing in Venezuela and had miraculously come home earlier that year. Wyatt had seen him at a few services, but they had never been formally introduced.

"Excuse me, sir." Lionel hurried toward Gideon. "Do you have any money? I lost my job last week, and my rent is due. If I don't pay, my family . . ."

Wyatt shook his head. Lionel didn't *have* a family. He was a loner. But Gideon didn't know that, and Lionel was obviously trying to prey upon his sympathies.

"Come with me," Gideon said. "I can't promise money, but I can get you food and some other necessities that may help."

"Come on, man." Lionel stepped closer. "My family will be out in the cold if I don't pay."

Wyatt clamped his jaw. He was tempted to intervene, to tell Gideon that Lionel had no family but that he would indeed be out in the cold if he didn't get money. If Gideon was anything like his father and the other members of his church, he would be sympathetic enough to Lionel's circumstances, even if he was alone.

Gideon reached into his jacket pocket before pulling back. "I'm sorry. Food and supplies are all I have to offer."

Lionel's nostrils flared, and his fists clenched. Wyatt frowned and stepped forward. Lionel was not a violent person, but he was desperate. Wyatt wasn't sure what he would do.

"You're lying," Lionel said. "I saw that car you pulled up in. You're not hurting for cash."

Gideon closed his eyes. His shoulders drooped in a deep sigh. Wyatt sympathized. It was possible that Gideon would like to help, but he truly did not have any money on hand to offer. It was not his fault Lionel had been waiting for him that day.

"I really don't have what you need on me," Gideon insisted. "But come to the church and—"

"What has the church ever done for us?" Lionel snarled. "They pull in here after things start getting bad, trying to make it right. But we all know this church has members at Lakeside that are well off enough to help us all out. Where are they?"

Okay, that's enough. If Lionel escalated further, things could get ugly. Besides, Wyatt didn't want Gideon thinking that he felt the same way about the church as Lionel did, especially since he was a member. He hurried past the crackling fire and eased up to Lionel's side.

"Aw, leave him alone, Lionel." Wyatt grabbed his friend's shoulder. "It's not the boy's fault."

"No. I said, where are they? Hiding in their towers and their fancy houses, waiting for the crime to bust us in the Brooks down to dust."

"Sir, that—" Gideon started.

"Church won't help our families stay out of the cold! My landlord's in the mob's pocket, man. He'll kick us out the day I don't pay rent! He's not gonna give me a second chance 'cause if he does, the mob's gonna put a bullet in his brain instead of money in his wallet. My friend here, he just lost his job, too. How long until he's in the same situation?"

Wyatt sensed Gideon's gaze boring into him, so he dropped his eyes. *He didn't need to know that.* Pastor Jeff already knew about Wyatt's joblessness and was trying to help him. There was no reason to burden Gideon, as well.

"I understand, sir," Gideon said. "It's an injustice—"

"Well, then, why don't somebody do something about it? Huh?" Lionel pushed Gideon's shoulder. Wyatt hurried to grab his friend's arm, but Lionel was unwavering. "Where's the cops? Oh, that's right, they're up at Lakeside defending the rich people that pay for this church and letting us rot."

Gideon took a step back and stumbled off the sidewalk into the street. He held up his hands. Wyatt hoped Lionel did not take the gesture as a preparation to retaliate. The last thing Wyatt wanted to do was deck his friend. Gideon was not in the wrong, though; and if Lionel fought him, Wyatt would protect the pastor's son. From what he knew about the past year of Gideon's life, he had suffered enough.

"I'm sorry." Gideon took a step back onto the sidewalk. "I really am. If I could fix it by myself, I would, but . . . "

Lionel scoffed. "If everyone who said that would get together and actually do something about it, maybe things would get solved around here."

That was unfair in Wyatt's eyes. The people of Refuge Church really were doing their best. Wyatt had seen it himself. Several families had donated meals and groceries in the time since Wyatt had lost his job. They were doing their part. Wyatt, too, had tried to do his part as the Crusader. It did not help financially, but it kept people somewhat safer. Unfortunately, none of that would ever be enough for Lionel. He would never be happy until he was wealthy enough to make it out of the Brooks for good.

"You're right." Gideon reached into his pocket. "Here. I have twenty bucks on me. Not enough, but maybe if anyone else can help you, you can put it together and pay rent. Or at least give it to your landlord as a down payment or something."

Lionel shook his head. "Thanks. But he don't do down payments."

"You can still come to the church, you know."

"Nah." He returned to the fire. "I'm good."

Wyatt traded glances with Gideon. There was hurt in the young man's eyes, and Wyatt gave him a shrug that he hoped came off as apologetic. Then, he backed toward the fire to be with Lionel. Gideon trudged away with a sigh. Wyatt watched him go with a pang of sympathy. But then, that sympathy blossomed into something stronger. Hope.

He saw something in Gideon. There was a compassion evident in the young man's voice as he spoke to Lionel. But that compassion was matched with sharp conviction. Sorrow and fury were mixed in Gideon's tense shoulders and fiery gaze as he took in the refuse-littered streets and the obscene graffiti marring the walls around them. In Gideon, Wyatt saw a determination to do good. It was the same kind of determination that had led Wyatt to become the Crusader. Gideon clearly saw the injustice of the Brooks; and in his eyes, Wyatt saw that Gideon was not the type to turn away from injustice.

Maybe I'm not alone anymore. Wyatt did not know what Gideon could—or would—do. What he did know was that change came when people decided to stop sitting around and watching and instead rose to take action. The Brooks had been hopeless for a long time . . . but until recently, there had been no one willing to do what it took to make things right.

Wyatt was willing. The Crusader would make that change, even if it took years. And if Wyatt's feeling about Gideon Turner was right, then the Crusader would not be alone anymore.

Change was coming. Not even the strongest forces for evil could stop that anymore.

END

JAKE TYSON

" . . . an action-packed superhero story
that shows the darkness so that the Light
shines even brighter."
—JASON JOYNER,
author of *Rise of the Anointed: Launch*
and *Fractures*

VIGILANTE'S
LIGHT

NEXT IN *THE VINDICATORS* SERIES...

The perfect orange globe of the sun contrasted beautifully with the purple sky as it met with the horizon. Gideon admired the view from the window of the rescue plane with new appreciation. He had all but given up hope on ever seeing a sight like this again. It was all he could do not to stare at the sun.

His gaze wandered downward to the earth far below. Directly below, the lights of a small town fell into shadow as the sun sank ever lower. It was the largest sign of modern civilization he'd seen in months.

It was all so amazing, and he had taken it for granted his whole life. Not anymore.

Something moved next to Gideon, and he swung his head around. The agent who'd greeted him, the one who'd been on the radio, was kneeling beside Gideon's seat. He had introduced himself as Agent Ross.

"We'll be landing in about half an hour. Your parents are already waiting for you at the landing strip."

"Thank you." Agent Ross started to get up, and Gideon grabbed his arm. "Anyone else?"

"What's that?"

"Is anyone else there?"

"I'm not sure, son. I made sure there wouldn't be a whole crowd of people—there won't be any media or anything—but I don't know who your parents brought with them."

"Okay. Thank you."

Ross nodded and moved back to his seat. Gideon slowly let his gaze return to the window. He could just see his reflection in the Plexiglas. He needed a haircut and a shave. Even before his captivity, he'd had a beard, but it had always been neatly trimmed—Jolie had called it "attractively scruffy." It was way too bushy now. His blond hair was long past his shoulders, tangled and matted. His long-sleeved blue Henley shirt had a few holes in it, and his gray pants and black shoes were tattered and dirty.

He didn't care. Once, he would've died if Jolie had seen him like this. Now, he just wanted to hug her and never let her go. He hoped she had come to the landing strip with his parents.

Before he'd gone down to Venezuela, he'd bought an engagement ring. He'd planned to propose to her upon his return to the States. That had been a year ago.

Gideon sighed, closed his eyes, and leaned back in his seat. Shouts and gunfire echoed in his ears. Pinpricks crawled all over his skin, and he shivered. How long it would take to erase the memories of that awful year?

He opened his eyes. On the horizon, he could see Sojourn City, Michigan jutting out into Lake Superior. *Home.*

When Gideon had first been grabbed by the guerrillas on his third day in Venezuela, he'd been sure they were going to kill him. He'd mentally said his goodbyes to all his loved ones and prayed they would find peace and comfort after they heard about his death. He'd given up on ever seeing Sojourn City again. But the guerrillas hadn't killed him, and his prayers had changed to pleading God to send someone to rescue him.

Finally, he was coming home.

Memories of the past year rushed through Gideon's mind, and he struggled to push them out. *The end of a rifle cracked against his skull, and then he fell and felt another impact as his head hit the ground. Leather straps curled tightly around his wrists, holding him to the table. Tubes and needled pierced his arms; a strange device weighed down his head. A gunshot echoed. "No!"*

He snapped back to reality. All that was over.

The plane descended. Gideon took a deep breath, ran a hand through his hair, and tried to settle down. He should be able to relax now; he was free, and he was home. If only it were that easy. Every little sound or movement triggered his fight-or-flight reaction. Maybe a good night's sleep in his own bed would help. Maybe if he could pretend things were normal for long enough, he'd start to believe it.

Maybe.

The plane jolted as it touched the ground. Gideon jumped, but the federal agents were all relaxed, calmly waiting for the plane to stop. He sighed and forced himself to sit straight and still. It seemed like hours before the plane finally rolled to a complete stop. Gideon looked out the window. Several people stood on the landing strip, but it was almost completely dark now, so he couldn't tell who.

There was movement in Gideon's peripheral. He turned. Agent Ross was standing next to him again. The agent placed a hand on Gideon's shoulder.

"You're home, son. Let's go."

Gideon unbuckled his seatbelt and stood. He didn't have any luggage to grab and this wasn't a commercial airliner anyway. There was no line to the exit ramp; the other agents were still in their seats. He

could go now, get off the plane, and run and hug his family. He took
a deep breath, steadied himself, and took it one step at a time.

As he reached the ramp, the cool spring air washed over his face.
He closed his eyes and smiled. It was so different from the hot, sticky
air of Venezuela. He'd almost forgotten. He took one step down the
ramp, then another. The figures on the strip were approaching at a
brisk walk, and one of them—his mother, Tasha—sped up to almost
a run. He took the last three steps down to the pavement.

And then she was on him. She embraced him, and the feeling of a
warm, loving contact with another human being rushed through Gideon.
He squeezed, hugging his mother as tightly as he ever had. Tears welled
in his eyes and as he blinked, they streamed down his cheeks.

"Mom," he whispered.

"Thank God you're safe!"

"I am." He squeezed her again. "I love you."

"I love you, too."

Gideon looked up past her. There were four others behind her: his
father, Matthew, younger brother, Wes, former youth pastor, Jeff, and
best friend, Dean. *No Jolie?* Gideon pushed the disappointment aside;
he would worry about her later. After another ten seconds, he released
his mother and moved to his dad.

"Gideon," his father rumbled.

The breath rushed from Gideon's lungs as his dad grabbed him in
a huge bear hug and squeezed. Gideon grinned and felt more tears on
his face. He hugged back and cried onto his father's shoulder. He felt
his brother, Wesley, move up beside him. Reluctantly, he released his
father and turned to hug Wes.

"I knew you weren't dead," Wes said. "You're too tough!"

Gideon grinned and ruffled Wes' hair, which was a few shades darker than Gideon's own. As he stepped back from his brother, he turned to look at Dean. Gideon's best friend pushed his curly, out-of-control brown hair out of his face and stepped toward Gideon.

"What Wes said." Dean grinned and hugged Gideon.

Pastor Jeff stepped forward and put a hand on Gideon's shoulder. "I never stopped praying for you, Gideon. I'm so glad you're safe."

When Gideon finally stepped back out of the hug, he felt suddenly awkward. What now? Where did they go from here? Judging from the way Dad shuffled his feet, Wes kicked a pebble, and Mom looked down at her hands, none of them really knew, either.

"Can we go home?" Gideon asked. "I could sleep for a week."

"Right." Dad chuckled. "Let's go."

* * *

The ride back to the house was much more opulent than Gideon had expected. Dean's family business, Sterling Enterprises, had provided a limousine for the Turners' use. The four of them, along with Dean, had piled into the back seat, while Pastor Jeff left in his own car on church business. As the car pulled out of the airport parking lot, Gideon stared out the window, taking in the familiar sights of his home.

"What have I missed?" he asked.

There was a long silence. Gideon looked away from the window. Dad and Mom were looking at each other as if unsure who should answer. Finally, Dad turned to Gideon and leaned forward.

"A lot." His father put a hand on Gideon's shoulder. "For starters, the upper class have moved offshore completely and onto the lake."

Sojourn City had been an experiment of sorts: what if the wealthy and the destitute ran the city together—upper, middle, and lower classes alike living in harmony? The business center of Sojourn City, along with the high-rises and skyscrapers that the wealthy called home, had literally been built on the lake—a floating platform built by Sterling Enterprise's science division. But most of the upper class had lived on the shore of the lake, near to the lower class. They had done what they could to provide jobs, resources, and supplies for the poor.

Gideon had always felt it was a bad idea and would eventually go awry. It looked like he was right.

"What else?"

"There's been a lot of crime growing in the poorer parts of town—people have started calling it the Brooks because they're on the riverfront. That's led to the majority of the police force moving toward the shore to protect the upper class. They would deny it, of course, but they're being paid off."

Gideon clenched his jaw. "And Jolie?"

Again, Mom and Dad exchanged glances. "Jolie is one of the few officers who's remained in the Brooks. There's a handful of precincts left there; they're doing the best they can."

"That's why she wasn't here," Mom said. "She's on patrol."

That was a relief. At least she hadn't moved on. But at the same time, Gideon felt a sudden wave of nervousness and protectiveness. He wanted to go out and find her and drag her to safety. *She can take care of herself. Which one of us just spent a year in captivity, again?*

He thought back to the inexplicable blinding light blasting from his hands. He shoved the memory aside, unwilling to think about what he'd become.

"Is there any hope of recovery?" he asked.

"Right now, we're doing what we can for the poor," Dad said. "We've opened two new church campuses in the Brooks and we're using them to supply food and shelter. Pastor Jeff is the lead pastor at one of them, and he's doing great work. But to actually drive out the crime?" He sighed. "I'm afraid it's a slow process."

Gideon slammed his open palm against his knee. Couldn't *anything* go right? From captivity to a freak of nature to a city overrun by crime . . . *God, what can I do to stop it?*

* * *

When Gideon woke up, the sun was shining through the window at his back and to the left of his bed. He inhaled, rolled onto his back, and slowly let his breath out. He felt . . . refreshed. He wondered how long he'd slept. It hadn't been later than eight or nine o' clock when he'd gotten home. What time it was now?

He'd dropped into bed as soon as he possibly could. He'd hardly waited for the car to stop before opening the door and trudging up the sidewalk toward the house. As his father had unlocked the door, Gideon had been tempted to just crash on the couch, but he ultimately decided that he needed his own bed. He forced himself upstairs, mumbling good night to everyone, and he barely remembered entering his room or collapsing onto his bed.

He tried to sit up—and pain racked his body. He grimaced. All the beatings and prodding he'd suffered had finally caught up to him. The adrenaline from running, followed by the relief of rescue, had dulled the pain. But now, it hit him full-force.

Slowly, he pushed himself upright. Every nerve in his body seemed to scream at him. He looked at the alarm clock beside his bed. It was just after noon. He took a breath to steady himself and swiveled to put his feet on the floor. The house was too big to call out and hope someone was nearby; he'd have to get downstairs himself.

Gideon grabbed the edge of his bed and pushed. When he was on his feet, he shuffled toward the door. He realized he hadn't even taken off his shoes before he'd fallen asleep. He was still in the same raggedy clothes he'd been rescued in. But he didn't feel like changing—not right now.

He reached for the door. The brass knob was cool on his hand—cooler than pretty much anything else he'd touched in the past year. He opened the door, went out, down the hall, and to the stairway. His mother was in the living room below, sitting on the couch facing the fireplace, her back to him, talking to . . .

He steadied himself on the banister.

"Jolie." He hardly recognized his own voice.

Her head swiveled around, and she beamed. "Gideon!"

"Are you okay?" Mom asked.

He gritted his teeth and nodded. "Yeah, but I . . . think I need a doctor."

Jolie's smile disappeared. Both women jumped off the couch and ran up the stairs to his side. Jolie got there first; as she reached him, he leaned into her for support.

"I'll call Doctor Edwin right now to let him know we're coming," Mom said. "Let's get you down to the car."

Gideon looked at Jolie as they walked down the stairs. Her dark hair and almost-black eyes contrasted beautifully with her pale skin.

She was everything he'd remembered, and despite the pain, he wanted to just stand there and relish being in her presence again.

"Hi," he said.

"Hi." She smiled again. "I'm so glad you're home."

"Me . . . too."

The stairs were an agonizing affair, but finally, they reached the floor. Jolie helped Gideon out the door while his mother grabbed her cell phone and keys off one of the side tables. Gideon groaned as he stumbled out the door and to the car. Jolie sat beside him in the back seat, and he slumped against her.

"I love you," she said.

"I love you, too." He gingerly wrapped his arm around her and gave her the best hug he could manage. "I never thought I'd see you again."

"I knew I'd see you again." Jolie beamed. "I never doubted it."

Gideon smiled. As they drove to the hospital, the two of them just sat there, resting in each other's arms. Gideon tried to ignore the pain racking his body, but it seemed to keep reminding him, *I'm still here.*

It seemed like forever, but they finally reached East Regional Hospital, where Dr. Edwin worked—where Gideon himself had worked, before his trip. Carl Edwin was a member of Refuge Church, where Gideon's father pastored, and he had assured them that he was on call for them whenever they needed him. Jolie helped Gideon out of the car, while his mother ran to get a wheelchair.

Edwin was waiting for them just inside the hospital, and he led them back to an examination room.

"Let him lie down," Edwin said.

Gideon held out a hand, and Jolie helped him to his feet. She brought him over to the bed and he pulled himself up. Edwin stepped up beside Gideon and began his examination.

Suddenly, Gideon worried that somehow, Edwin would find out about the light that had come from Gideon's hands. Would that be the kind of thing that would show up on any scans the doctor did? Even as a doctor himself, Gideon had no idea what had happened to his body, and no idea how it would manifest itself.

"He's definitely sustained some serious bruising," Edwin said. "Not surprising, all things considered. There are no signs of internal bleeding, though. I'd like to do an x-ray to make sure he doesn't have any broken bones."

Gideon hoped that was all Edwin found.

* * *

Hours later, Gideon was able to go home. Dr. Edwin had prescribed him painkillers, but other than that he'd said Gideon would recover with time. None of his injuries should cause future problems, provided he didn't aggravate them before they had a chance to heal properly, and he didn't have any broken bones, miraculously.

And he hadn't said anything about any anomalies. As far as Gideon knew, Edwin hadn't discovered his secret—whatever it was.

Sitting on the couch back at his parents' house, leaning against Jolie's shoulder, Gideon thought that maybe his life could finally go back to having some semblance of normalcy now.

Maybe.

For more information about
Jake Tyson
&
The Vindicators Series

please visit:

www.creatingforcreator.wordpress.com
www.facebook.com/jaketysonauthor96

For more information about
AMBASSADOR INTERNATIONAL
please visit:

www.ambassador-international.com
@AmbassadorIntl
www.facebook.com/AmbassadorIntl

If you enjoyed this book, please consider leaving us a review on
Amazon, Goodreads, or our website.

If it's true that "all comic novels must be about matters of life and death," *The Honest Atheist* obliges. This entertaining and thought-provoking tragicomedy provides clues to where our loss of public decency originates while telling a moving story of an unlikely friendship between an atheist and an evangelical Christian. Part crime story and part apologetic treatise, *The Honest Atheist* is a comedic and binge-worthy work.

After Catherine Reed's husband dies, she moves back home in order to accept a new position as the teacher for the town's one-room schoolhouse. Samuel Harris has suffered his own loss and guilt has burdened him ever since. When his old flame comes back to town, he wonders if they can find healing together . . .

Sam Anthem has always been a team player, leading his Home Team on secret missions around the world. When he is forced on a vacation, he is introduced to a former covert ops soldier-turned pastor. But the vacation takes a turn when the Home Team comes under attack. As the team fights to stay alive against an unknown adversary, Sam begins to wonder if there is more to life than just the job. With his life on the line, Sam must decide between the job or his newfound faith and possible love.